Mountain Dew Trilogy II:

Cheat River Gang

By

Harold H. Milton

ISBN-13: 978-0692955468

ISBN-10: 0692955461

Printed in the United States of America

Printed by Janice Publishing

Other Books by Harold H. Milton: *The*

Appalachian Collection: Remembering

the Hill Country

The Treasure of the Hills

Water Baptism

The Conquest of Lonnie Dolan

Mountain Dew Trilogy I:

Revenue Man the Lonesome Traveler

Mountain Dew Trilogy II:

Cheat River Gang

Mountain Dew Trilogy III:

Nell's Sojourn

I, Janice, dedicate the Mountain Dew Trilogy to my mother, Nellie Agnes Romeo-Blanton. She was born February 1st, 1924 in Gypsy, West Virginia. She died at 36 years old of Leukemia on May 27, 1960 in Cleveland, Ohio. I was five. "Nell" as she liked to be called is mentioned towards the end of the Mountain Dew Trilogy, which is Harold Milton's 1st manuscript written over a twelve-year period that they had discussed together. This book was God planned.

Forever a Loyal Daughter

And grateful to our readers

Janice Louise Blanton

Nellie A Romeo

1940

Mother Nellie Agnes Blanton with daughter Janice Blanton

1955

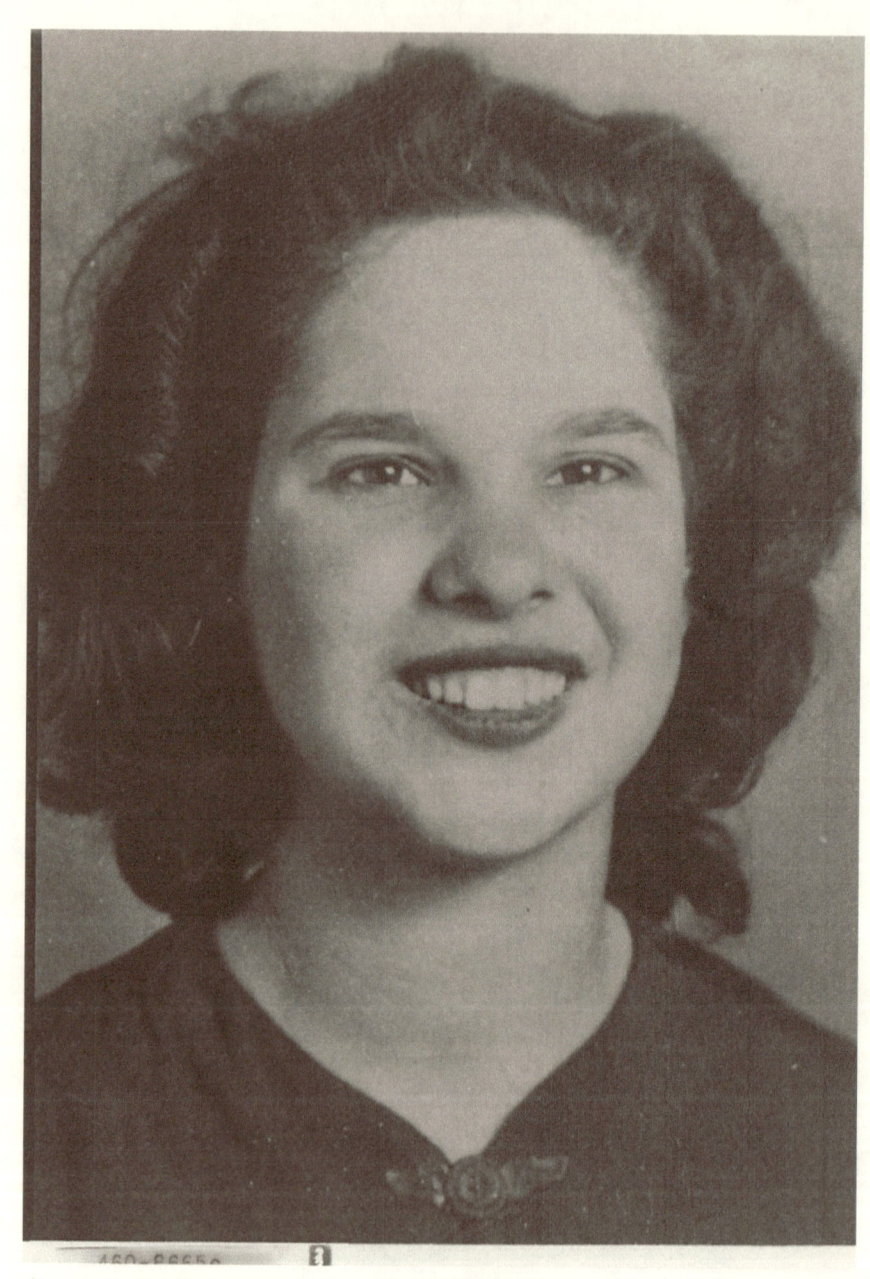

Nellie A Romeo

1938

Nellie Agnes Romeo-Blanton

Day of Baptism

Acknowledgement

Harold H. Milton's first book Mountain Dew was completed after twelve years while he was writing other novels and short stories. He began his ideas in the 1930s. He was German and born in Marietta, Ohio December 23rd, 1913, the only red haired son of Charles Henry Milton born February 10th, 1872 and whom passed away November 22, 1946 and Eva Marilla Farley born January 6th, 1885 and passing away April 1963. He had three older sisters named Hazel, Myrtle, Jewell, and one younger named Mary. They lived in a small cabin and had their education in a one room school house. Their poverty was severe and Harold was embarrassed to carry all five lunches to school in a basket.

During the Depression, Harold had to quit school in the eighth grade to help his father with farming and hunt Ginseng and yellowroot for profit. Harold loved these times with his father and they would have contests to see who would find the most herbs.

Together the family traveled and lived in West Virginia by pushing a dust covered wagon, often the wheels would get stuck in the mud or the wagon broke down. The Milton family played different musical instruments together to entertain parties and appear during celebrations in order to have food to eat. Harold moved to Cleveland, Ohio in his twenties and purchased a typewriter. He began writing and typing Mountain Dew over a 12-year period before and after he married Jane A.

Romeo. She became his character Jane Burton. Jane was born October 3rd, 1925 in Gypsy, West Virginia and died December 1986 in Cleveland. She was Dutch, Italian, and English. They were married over 44 years.

It was a cold winter day when I, Janice Louise Blanton, was born in Cleveland, Ohio on January 16th, 1955 to Nellie Agnes Romeo who was born February 1st, 1924 in Gypsy, West Virginia and Orville B. Blanton born July 18th, 1922 in Kentucky. The rule at Booth Memorial-a Salvation Army Hospital for unwed mothers was that you could live there your last trimester, you had to do chores and you had to relinquish your baby. Nellie took me home and my first crib was a dresser drawer for five months. She then married Orville and continued her waitress job while Harold and Jane babysat me from four months on. Five years later, my mother Nellie died of Leukemia at 36 years young and Harold agreed to raise me full time while my father Orville visited often until he died in 1966 at 43 years old of heart disease.

In 1960, Harold knocked on many doors and built a congregation to open a Church of Christ. We spent weekends walking thru the woods collecting ginseng that dried out in our attic and was sold. He loved to talk about his childhood days and speak German with his daughter, Nancy, who also died at nineteen years old of a brain tumor while in her second year at Cleveland State University. She was a lovely redhead and we loved each other as Sisters and laughed a lot and played tennis. The feeling of my being orphaned kept getting worse but Harold was there for me and it made us closer to be Father and Daughter. As children, Nancy and I were asked by him, "What do you girls want when my books hit it big?" Her answer was a white baby grand piano.

For forty years, he wrote and typed books that were wanted for publishing in New York. He never had the finances for this and Nancy's college loan and funeral expenses were high, though he continued writing. We lived together the last 12 years of his life.

With my encouragement, he completed his G.E.D. at 79 years old. I had a nice party and it made the newspaper and he planned to go to

College but we moved to a different home further away. He always wanted to see the Grand Canyon so in 1994, we went there. We stayed in Vegas. He liked that also and would imitate a robot dancing that he had seen in a show. He died at eighty-four years old as I held his hand in the hospital. I had saved his life over thirty times when he had chest pain. I was now an emergency room Registered Nurse working all departments, even up to 100 hours a week. As I watched Harold's passing, I was saddened that his departing was such a loss, for he knew his Bible word for word and was so nice, kind and smart. I inspired to become a Nurse at age eight and had taken care of him when he was very sick before and after a surgery in 1963. He had taken care of me also. Around 2000, I noticed his books under my stairwell and read some of it, however in 2012, I wanted to get them published and leave his fingerprints in the world.

It is now through my labor of love that I present to you're the writings of my second Father, Harold Homer Milton. As I now carry out his dream and pull back the curtain of time and the past, he smiles down from Heaven and becomes a known author. I can now sit back and listen to Nancy play on her white baby grand piano. His seven books are named *Mountain Dew Trilogy I, II, and III, The Treasure of the Hills, Water Baptism, The Conquest of Lonnie Dolan* and *The Appalachian Collection: Remembering the Hill Country.*

Fondly and with great honor,
Janice Louise Blanton

Note for the Lucky Reader

It is to be noted that the language used in this novel is spoken in the 1920's West Virginian style of speech. I have kept it this way to stay true to the memory of Harold H. Milton and his family, as well as to commemorate the history of the people and their culture. I have greatly enjoyed working with Janice Blanton on her endeavors. My hope is that, you, the reader of this novel enjoy the works that Harold and Janice have put all of their heart and soul into.

-Lyssa Barsda-

FOREWARD

The spell of the high hills comes back to me.
Again and again, I feel their calling. I need but to
close my eyes to be once more within their lofty
fastness. I see the ragged ridges running in endless
parallels; their crests oftentimes filmed with lacy
clouds. In memory, I see in my minds' eye the
many hued rainbows arching the valley at my feet.
While from my vantage viewpoint high on a
bulging slope, I can look straight across the top of
the rainbow to the soaring mountains beyond I see
the great forests, stretching magnificently on, and
on. The vast coves, the gigantic peak-like
formations thrusting their proud heads thousands
of feet into the heavens. Once more I traverse the
wide valleys; ford the crystal clear amber colored

rivers and streams and with hurrying steps bury myself deep within the recesses of a West Virginia woodland.

In my boyhood days, I lived in West Virginia. Not steadily, however, but upon more than one occasion. For a period, I went to school there.

In the late summer of 1935 I took a camping trip into the Cheat Mountains. While on that trip I fell in love with that wild high country. Many times, I slept 'neath the stars upon its mighty heights. Its' clear rushing streams and rivers fascinated me. The ways and customs of the people of this mountain-land were a revelation. Through the years new ideas and ways had seeped in from the outside. New laws and acts of Congress had left their mark upon their inherited way of life. They told me their old mode of life was fast becoming but a memory. Fondly the Old Timers told of the days that used to be, there in the mountains. Regretfully they acknowledged their passing.

Many trips I took into the mountains of West Virginia since my initial trip of 1935. Always I was shown every hospitality. Every time I would take my departure I was always urged to return, again and again.

The following story is purely fictional. In writing it I've depicted life in that upland country as its citizens informed me it once existed. Its plot, and characters, I have diligently strived to portray as true to life as I possibly could.

It has been my personal experience to find the mountaineer to be a man of honor. The possessor of an incomparable hospitality. Honest as the day is long. Embracing a down-to-earthiness that stems from an honest heart; a sincere regard for his fellow man.

However, aside from all these commendable qualities, if need be, the mountaineer can be an individual of an entirely different mien. Should the occasion so demand he will stand forth in terrible wrath and violently defend, and uphold, his beliefs and inherited ways and customs. He holds a great contempt for all those who would deal with him in a two-faced manner.

I salute the people of our mountain state. I am humbly grateful that at times in my past life I have been one of them.

In closing this forward, I proudly dedicated this book to my loving wife, Jane, a native West Virginian.

Sincerely yours,

Harold H. Milton

3466 East 119th street

Cleveland 20, Ohio

December 1952

Mountain Dew Trilogy II:

Cheat River Gang

By

Harold H. Milton

Mountain Dew Trilogy II:

Cheat River Gang

The month of October was extravagantly beautiful in the high country. Jack Frost painted with a prodigal hand the coves, the ridges, the draws, the valleys. He touched them all with his colorful brush. The maples had turned a bright gold, while the oaks had taken on a ruddy hue. The evergreens remained the same, save only for a darker, deeper, shade of green. The grass in the upland country had taken on the gray look of winter. Fall had come to the mountains. Squirrels were hurrying about gathering nuts and acorns like little misers. And the own lords of creation; mankind, was also preparing for the long dormant months ahead. In fact, all nature knew that the winter season was but weeks away, and prepared accordingly.

It had been a busy month and a happy one for the revenue man. He had gone down to Valley Head and had rented a post office box. He wrote to his superiors in Washington, D. C. explaining to him the reason for not contacting him sooner. And promised to keep in touch as time went by, but even as he wrote to Mr. Bain he knew his heart for the job, and all it pertained to was gone forever. While down at Valley Head he purchased a birthday present for Jane. It was a beautiful locket and matching bracelet set. When he gave it to her on her birthday, she received it with trembling hands. A deeply touching smile was on her face as she opened the package. How her eyes shone as she looked at them. How proudly she wore them to church the following Sunday. Later the happy girl crept into his arms in the evening twilight and gave him a lingering kiss as his reward for remembrance. Her father and mother and the Indian all remembered her on her birthday but she told Tom that she valued his gift above all others, and for many reasons.

He had gone to church every Sunday of that month and with each passing Sabbath his liking and appreciation of the grey old backwoods preacher increased. He was indeed a philosopher of life, and his straightforward way of looking at things and of making decisions was beyond gainsaying.

Tom had gone to work the week following the Sabbath he had first met Preacher Kane. His strength had gradually increased until by the time October had almost gone he felt nearly himself again. For a week now he and Jim had been cutting props. The scene of their activities was up a little draw that came down to the little valley where stood the big two-trunked walnut tree. The second growth timber of this little hollow was ideal for props. Scarcely none of the trees were more than a foot in diameter at the butt and rose in the air straight as broom handles. The young poplar they did not cut because Burton had said the prop inspector would not pass any props cut from soft wood. All types of oak were acceptable, together with ash, birch, hard maple, hickory and in fact all hard woods. They cut and trimmed out the long straight slender young trees and then with the span of miles, which Burton had bought for that purpose snaked them down onto the littler bottom for sawing into lengths and for splitting.

Tom took turns with the Indian at driving the young mules. He had no trouble with them, but compared with Debassius his knowledge and ability of handling horseflesh was sadly lacking. Jim could do wonders with the long-eared beasts of burden in his slow, easy, effortless way. He never spoke harshly to them, never tried to crowd, or overload them, and they in turn seemed to put forth an extra measure of effort to please him. They never offered to bite him, never tried to kick him, and Tom never saw one of those big long velvety ears laid down in anger while the Indian had hold of the lines. Always they were standing straight up, as perhaps they might be leaning backwards a little, as if listening for a gentle word, or for a soft spoken command. Jane said she didn't trust mules and gave them a wide berth. Her father left the handling of them entirely up to the two prop cutters, saying that he didn't want to mess things up for them, as he never considered himself a mule shinner.

One day in late October he came home at dusk and announced that the next day they would go bear hunting.

"Jim and Tom I been over in the big cove today," he said with flashing eyes. "And up close to the crest of that ridge over yonder found the partly eaten remains of four young ewes. The signs

around them dead sheep all point to bears. So oil

up the thirty-thirty tonight Jim cause' I predict

we'll be using it before this time tomorrow."

"Were there any tracks around the dead

ewes?" asked the Indian in his soft drawl.

"A few. But not plain. What I base my guess

on is the way they were killed. Their necks were

broken, all of them, and a bear could do that with

one swipe of his paw. Now if it had of been a

panther he would have jumped on their backs and

dragged them down, but not breaking their necks."

A thrill shot through Tom at the thought of what

the morrow would bring. He had been told that

bear hunting was not an uncommon thing in this

mountain country, and had always looked forward to the day when he might participate in one. At last this long hoped for event was about to take place.

"Will we ride behind the dogs?" he asked.

"We'll ride till we have to get off and walk," answered both the Indian and Burton. "Most generally those bears are wise to what hunters will do and they make for the thickest, roughest places they can find."

"Is Jane going with us," he inquired. "If she wants to she can," her father answered. "But I'll warn her she might expect a rough long hike. We'll no doubt hole them bears up back on the top of that hogback about five miles from here under that big laurel bed. An' then have to stand around with guns ready when the dogs go in and rout them out. When an old bear comes charging out he's dangerous." "Shore' is," put in Debassius, "and take my advice. If you-all don't drop him or her as the case may be, at the first two shots – well make fer' the closest tree, and waste no time getting' up it."

"If that's the case I don't think we had better let Jane go," said Tom.

"Tom you-all have the job of persuadin' her to stay at home then son, out of harm's way," observed the bearded giant, "And I wish you-all luck. But don't count on it. Haw, Haw."

"I've tried to talk her out of goin' with Lige and me on hunts before," put in Jim, "an' I'm here to say so far I've a perfect score – for failure that is."

"Well, I'll try," Tom said. "But I say only add to your score Jim. She could get badly hurt on a hunt like that. Does she carry a gun?"

"Oh yes," answered her father. "And knows how to use it, well as most men around here. I'm glad to say."

"Think I'll go in and see if she'll listen to reason," Tom said. And rising from his chair left the two-room cabin, where they had been discussing the hunt, and began walking toward the main cabin. He had gotten about halfway across the yard when he was hailed from the smaller cabin by the booming voice of the mountaineer. "Bell come back here. I've somethin' more to say," he called. Tom retraced his steps.

"I was just thinkin' just as you left," announced Burton, "that we'll spring this on Jane at supper. That way we'll all be present to sort of back one another up when she puts up a kick, which I'm sure she'll do."

"O. K. suits me," Tom replied.

They talked on making plans for the coming day. The Indian stepped to the door and looking at the clear October sky made mention of the fact they would probably have a nice fall day for their hunt.

"The sky is clear, the airs getting colder, an' my guess is there'll be a white frost on the ground by mornin'. It's better trailin' for the dogs if the ground is wet from a little shower. But to be safe we'll do our trailin' this time on frosty ground."

A light step was heard on the doorstep, and a knock on the door followed. "Supper's ready!" A voice called out. The door opened and in walked the owner of the voice they had heard. It was Jane. She looked at each in turn and smiled. How beautiful she is, Tom thought, and how I love her. She was dressed in a red cross-bared gingham dress, sweater, low-brown shoes, and anklets. Her head was covered with a large scarf because the fall air was nippy. Her cheeks were rosy and her brown eyes were wide and sparkling.

"Supper's ready," she again informed them.

"We'll be right there," her father answered in his deep voice.

"How was the prop cuttin' today Tom, and Jim?" she asked, turning to the two young men in question. "And how are those deceivin' mules behavin' themselves? Kick either of you yet?"

"Well now Jane," Jim began in his easy, slow, casual way. "They might of kicked Tom here but I sorts talked them out of the notion. Them long-ears behave good and obey me like a couple of kittens. Why you know that."

"I'll admit you do have a way with them. But don't trust a mule too far, 'cause they might forget to be good sometimes."

Turning to her father the girl asked him how he had found the stock over in the big cove, and if he had found any evidence of bears around and if so, were they doing any harm that he could see. Tom and Jim looked at Burton. He seemed to be squirming around in his seat. Presently he raised his eyes and gave her a hard grin.

"Yes, Janie girl, they've been causin' a bit of hell. Killed four ewes that I found, an' maybe more that I didn't see. Didn't look the cove over completely."

"Honestly daddy!" she exclaimed in a singing voice. "If that's the case we had better be going after them, don't you think?"

"Oh shore' hon!" the mountaineer said in positive tones. "We hunt for bear tomorrow, weather permittin'. But a vote among us three men has been taken and we agree it'll be a lot safer if you stay at home."

"Oh, fine," she told him with an uplifting of her glorious haired head, "Am I supposed to think otherwise? What then?"

"Well in that case Tom have'll try to make you see the light, after supper that is."

"Tom Bell," she turned to him in lofty fashion, "I've hunted bear with Daddy and Jim ever since Jim came to work for my father, and that has been all of five years this coming winter. And I'm here to say I've stayed up with them in a hunt and never got in their way when the game was finally cornered."

"Nuff' said right this minute on the subject about who's goin' and who's stayin'," boomed out the giant Burton.

"I'm hungry enough right now to eat a bear myself, so let's go an' eat our supper before it gets cold," so saying he rose from his chair and putting on a light jacket walked from the cabin.

Giving Tom and Jim a lingering look Jane walked at her fathers' heels out the door. They glanced at one another, raised their eyebrows, then shrugging their shoulders, they grinned and strode after Jane and her father.

Mrs. Burton greeted the young men pleasantly and at once began putting the hot food on the table. Jane silently assisted her.

Nothing was mentioned at the supper table about the forth coming bear hunt. The conversation was commonplace, and pertained only to ordinary daily events. Soon as the repast was finished however, then abruptly the small talk ended. Jane looked up from her last bite of pumpkin pie and calmly stated to her mother that her father, Tom and Jim, together with herself was going bear hunting the next day. Burton rolled out a low laugh at this, and glanced knowingly at Tom. Debassius did likewise. Mrs. Burton seemed not to have heard her daughter right for all the interest and concern she manifested.

"Well that will probably be excitin'," she quietly stated, "I suppose the usual arguments have been dragged out against your goin' no doubt, and as usual I know you're just as settled and convinced in your heart you're goin' along come what may. Am I right?"

"Positively, mother dear," Jane answered. "Dad gave Tom the job of tryin' to talk me into stayin' at home, where I would be safe and sound. An' I'm waitin' to hear his argument on why I should be left out of the fun."

"Jane, I honestly believe you would be much safer at home. Suppose a bear was to break cover and charge you when the dogs were pushing it? How do you know the furious animal would be shot and stopped in time to keep it from mauling you up and clawing you frightfully?"

"I don't know Tom, but I'm willin' to take the chance. I've always gone bear huntin' with father and Jim and I don't intend to quit because you-all feel squeamish," and the highland girl looked at Bell with a belligerent attitude. He tried another approach.

"Then again there's the element of keeping up with us men," he told her seriously. "And not lagging behind and maybe getting lost. You see it wouldn't be fair to you if we run off and leave you by yourself and then to stay at the pace you'll be able to maintain would spoil the hunt. So that wouldn't be fair to us men either. Don't you think so Jane?"

"If keeping up with you wonderful hikers is your main worry then let me put your mind at rest right now. Durin' all the years I went out huntin' with Daddy and Jim, I have always kept right up with the rest," turning to her father Jane looked at him squarely in the eye. "Tell this man how I've hunted every fall for bear and also tell Mr. Bell that I've still the first time to come home with as much as a scratch. Personally Tom, I think you will have trouble taking the pace we will set. You're still soft from last month. An' I know what I'm sayin' when I say an old bear is a tough customer to keep close to. Especially when the dogs are pushing it. Do you-all think you'll be able to keep up yourself?"

"Well now Jane and Tom," Burton interposed. "I see you-all air' havin' quite an interestin' time tryin' to discredit each other from taking' in the hunt. So if I'm allowed to make my private opinion known, I would say you two take in the hunt, an' sort of keep each other company.

When you both fall behind, What you say Jim?"

"Shore' reckon' they'll have to," Debassius replied in his tranquil easy way. "If the dogs put any bears up trees we'll wait until you-all have arrived on the scene of action before unlimbering the old Winchester."

"Looks like I've been overruled Jane," laughed Tom, "and I'll say I'm glad to see you go but for one thing."

"What's that?" she asked him.

"I'm worried you might get hurt some way, and I can't help feeling that way," he said solemnly. She laughed gaily and rising from the supper table soon had the dishes cleaned away. During the entire time Tom had been trying to get Jane to agree to stay at home when the three men went on the bear hunt, Mrs. Burton had sat quietly by and had smiled occasionally at Jane and Tom's debate. Now she arose and helped with doing up the supper dishes. Soon they were done. During the time Jane and her mother were doing the supper dishes, the three men had discussed the coming hunt pro and con. All angles were taken into consideration. After a while the Indian rose from his seat and said he would be going over to the cabin he and Tom shared. "I'm sort of fagged out and I've got to oil up my gun and sharpen my knife before I turn in. So I better be getin' at it. Comin' Tom?"

"Pretty soon now," Bell answered.

"I think I'll go for a little walk. That is if you'll go with me Tom," Jane said. "I haven't been on a walk in the cool fall night air yet this year. It's Halloween time and there's a big round moon just creeping up over the ridge back of Mingo. Daddy do you-all mind if Tom an' me take a little stroll? It's only eight-thirty. Not good bed time till at least another hour yet."

"Talk all you-all want to," rumbled the mountaineer. "Think I'll read awhile then turn in. I got enough walkin' for myself today over there in the cove. Remember if you-all air' goin' to keep within hearin' distance of them dogs tomorrow you had better hit the hay early. We'll be getin' started by gray daylight."

When Jane asked Tom to walk with her he immediately accepted the invitation. How his heart leaped at the thought of strolling in the moonlight with this big eyes, beautiful girl. Debassius gave them an overlook from his jet black eyes and turning round strode out the door, closing it softly behind him.

"I'll only be a minute getin' my coat." Jane said brightly, and straightway stepped into the huge living room to a built in clothes closet and took down her new winter coat of a dark green color with a brown fur collar. Her father had bought it for her birthday. Tom excused himself for a moment to go over to the two-roomed cabin and put on a coat. The Indian was busily oiling the high-powered rifle he always kept in the cabin. An eight-inch blade hunting knife lay cold and glittering in the lamp light by his side.

"Have a nice stroll," he said in a cool, easy drawl. And looking up from his work gave the revenue man a lopsided grin. Tom thanked him and walked out into the yard, wondering what lay in the Redman's' heart, and what was behind the queer look he had given him and Jane when she had asked him to go with her for a walk. Manlike he reasoned that it was very possible that the Indian was in love with his lovely girl himself. She had told him that day they had gone fishing that Debassius was only a good friend. But just because she looked upon Jim as only a friend was no proof that he held her emotionally in like manner.

Striving to put thoughts of this order from his mind, he walked across the yard and rapped lightly on the living room door. Jane opened the door almost immediately and telling her parents she wouldn't be gone long stepped out upon the steps beside Tom.

She smiled up at him in her roguish way taking his arm they swung round the cabin and into the road leading down to Mingo.

"I thought it would be nice to take a little walk this evening Tom," she told him in a half apologetic tone of voice. "Hope you-all aren't too tired to go."

"When I am with you Janie girl, I forget all thoughts of fatigue," he answered and squeezed her arm in emphasis. They walked on down the road slowly. The big late October moon was scarcely an hour high above the timbered ridges to the east. The dark trees bordering the roadway stood stark and bare in its' silvery light. Their naked trunks and branches threw weird ghostly shadows on the stony road. The heavy fall frosts and light breezes had put the leaves to bed days ago. Only a few clung tenaciously to the branches, as if reluctant to say farewell to the mother who bore them. The somber mountain hemmed in this small stream where dwelt the Burton family in a protecting manner. In any direction one would care to look was to be seen the might ridges and hogbacks climbing into the sky.

Jane and Tom climbed a gentle rise in the roadway. To the right bordering the stream bank, a hive of gnarled old red oaks stood. At some time in the past, the mountain farmer had left an eight-foot log of smallish diameter lying beneath one of the giant old trees. This cube of slowly decaying wood made an admirable seat and resting place. The revenue man had come often to this cool inviting spot during the weeks of his convalescence. Jane had accompanied him here on more than one occasion. So now as the slowly strolling couple came abreast of this retreat it seemed but only natural that they should turn aside into the dark silver streaked shadows, cast by the aged oaks, and take a seat upon the log.

"May I put my arms around you?" Tom asked the girl seated by his side.

"You may Mr. Bell," she replied. "Perhaps I'll stay warm if you do. It's cold out this evening. Don't you think so?"

"It is chilly that's for sure. But if you're cold I'll put my other arm around you. Are you cold?"

"Not that cold yet. But you never can tell," she answered with a low laugh.

"Jane have you changed your mind about going on that hunt tomorrow?"

"Not at all I haven't, and I'm not about to either."

"Yes but suppose you should get hurt of something?"

"I never have yet," she flashed out.

"That's no reason to say you never will. But I hope to God you never do."

Turning around so that she faced him squarely she looked up into his face. It was in shadow cast by his hat. Nevertheless, she looked longingly at that shaved face. Presently she spoke.

"Tom why don't you want me to go with you

and daddy and Jim tomorrow? Is it because you're afraid I might get hurt or is it because you're afraid I might prove to be a burden?"

"You a burden – never."

"Well why is it then?" she queried.

"You know my real reason," he burst out painfully.

"You tell me Tom. I'm forgetful as can be."

"I won't say," he returned with growling voice.

"Is it because you-all care for me?" she

whispered.

"You know I do girl."

"How much would you care if I was to get hurt Tom? A lot?" softly came the question.

His answer was a groan. Then tightening his arm around her shoulders he drew her close against his breast. Reaching down with his left hand he tilted back her head until her upturned face was just below his. His voice was heavy with emotion when he spoke. "I love you, I love you, Jane Burton. That's why I'm concerned about your safety. And I would never forgive myself if I was to take you along on a dangerous hunt like that and you was to get hurt understand?" She weakly nodded her head, but didn't try to stir from his grasping embrace. The revenue man couldn't resist any longer the magnetic lure of those sweet lips just inches below his own. He groaned again. Then suddenly he seemed to throw off that which had held him. Bowing his head slightly he rained passionate kisses upon that sweet mouth. Her arms came creeping up round his neck to lock there.

"Oh, Jane, Jane," ground the man aloud. "You torture me and torment me, you heartless girl. When I am only trying to protect you from harm you laugh and scoff at what I say and do. There's times when I'm tempted to think you don't love me at all."

Her arms only tightened around his neck if

that could be considered an answer. Presently her clasping arms released their grips and slid down off his shoulders. She seemed to droop and sag in his arms. Her action amazed Tom. Where was the lighthearted girl of this evening? He had sensed these moody spells ever since the day they had gone fishing. Of late Jane would seem gay and carefree as could be one day and would snap a person's head off the next if she was crossed in any way.

"Tom you-all will have to believe what you will about me," she finally told him. "I can't help it. But I know how I feel about everything that has happened between us. Someday maybe you'll know differently. I hope and pray so anyway."

Tom's heart leaped at that certain something in her voice. Rising from the log, where they sat, he walked a few paces away under the age old oaks. The girl sat in a small huddled figure on the log. He retraced his steps to her side, and again clasped her lax figure in this arms. Bending his face into her hair that stuck out from her head scarf about her ears he whispered many sweet things to her.

The big round moon hung low in the sky over the timbered country. They had sat an hour up on that log. The chill of the late October evening was beginning to make itself felt. Rising again from his seat Tom grasped Jane by the shoulders. She threw back her head and looked up at him with deep shadowy eyes. He slowly pulled her to her feet.

"My dear little girl. We'll have to be going back home. And remember this darling, tomorrow when we get that bear or bears cornered up my paramount wish is for your safety and well-being. Because you see, I love you."

"All right Tom. I'll always remember that," was her reply in a weak strained manner. "Let's be strolling back. We want to get a good night's rest, because tomorrow'll be plenty rough an' tough. An' Tom Bell," she added spiritedly, "don't you-all ever for a minute think I'm heartless. If I thought, you really meant that I would feel like hauling off and slapping you good and hard."

"Oh come now Janie, you know I was only talking to hear my head roar. I'm firmly convinced in my heart that you're the kindest, and best, and sweetest, and also the most beautiful girl I have ever known. And to add to all that I love you. So now go ahead and slap me."

"Alright I will," came her reply. Quickly she swung both arms wide and bringing her hands swiftly round brought them up against his face both at the same time. But there was no force behind them when they came up against his cheeks. Pressing her small cool hands firmly there, she raised herself on tip-toe and kissed him lingeringly on the lips.

"There you-all are Mr. Tom. Didn't I tell you

I would slap you? Now you'll believe I'm as good as my word. And if that doesn't convince you I'll do it again." She spoke with a half break in her voice, and seemed to be struggling for words. Some deep strong emotion was raging inside her breast. Of this the man standing before her was positive. Her hand had trembled against his face when she pretended to slap him.

"Jane Burton, do you love me?" abruptly he shot the question at her.

Before answering him, her head cropped for a moment, during which time her face was lost in shadow. When at last her face was again turned up to his how white and strained it looked in the silvery moonlight. Then slowly, haltingly, her answer came.

"Oh, Oh, Tom. Why must I be made to answer that question? I can only it is. You-all have kindled a fire within my heart the like of which I never before experienced. Its heaven to have you hold me in your arms and kiss me the way you do. I've never felt about anyone before like I feel about you. But I want so very much to be sure. I've opened my heart to you Tom. Is there anything in your heart that we should talk about. Have you-all made a clean breast of everything? I mean girls you may have known in the past, and might still not of forgotten completely. Or anything that might have some bearing on our future happiness together if we should up and get married? Is there anything you-all want to tell me, something maybe you would like to talk about?"

Inwardly the revenue men withered. Here was the call from the lips of the girl he loved to be honest with her as she was being honest with him. Again he must play the hypocrite, the liar, the deceiver, and lie to the honest hearted girl standing before him. At that moment how he hated the stinking job of revenue man, and hated himself just as cordially for becoming involved with anything like it. Averting her face he replied to her query in as natural a manner as he could summon at the moment.

"No Jane honey, I've nothing to tell you at this time. Maybe I'll have something to talk about with you in the future. And if I do rest assured I'll tell you everything. Will that be O.K for now dearest? I promise not to plague you with any more direct questions in the future. But I do believe dear girl that there's something ahead for you and I. Happiness I mean. But let's go home now honey. Or your father will be out looking for me with a gun for keeping you out in this cold fall air. If you get a cold from this, I deserve to be slapped and kicked and lots of things."

Without another word they walked out from the dark shadows under the ancient trees and started up the stony road for home. Barely a word was spoken between them as they slowly walked along. Tom had his arm around her, and she had the hand of that arm tucked in her coat pocket on the opposite side. Her small well shaped hand was also inside the roomy pocket clutching his hand.

She leaned against him as they strolled along.

Eventually they came to the large cabin, which was her home. Coming up through the yard, she stopped in the shadows close under the edge of the cabin. Then suddenly she twisted round inside the circle of his right arm and threw both her arms around him. Instinctively his arms went round the clinging girl. Her head lay against his chest for a moment, then was lifted so that her upturned lips almost touched his own. He could feel the warm breath from her half open mouth against his face. Passionately he kissed that half open mouth, feeling its' trembling response all the while. Things a man says to the girl he dearly loves whispered against that intoxicating mouth. Her answer was a straining against him, a tighter clasp of arms and an upward pushing of her pale oval face. When at last her arms dropped to her side she murmured a barely audible "Good night Tom" and quickly stepping round the edge of the cabin into the light of the big sailing room, walked to the door of the large living room and quietly let herself inside.

With dragging steps, the revenue man approached the door of the two room cabin he shared with the Indian. Softly he let himself inside, and quietly undressing crept into bed. He and Debassius each had a bed to themselves, for which he was thankful. A lantern burned with a low turned flame on a chair beside his bed. He heard the Indian turn in bed in the next room. When cold weather really hit the high country both beds would be put into the room containing the huge open fireplace.

Sleep was slow in closing his eyes that night. His watch said ten-thirty when he had gone to bed and he estimated it was midnight or later before he slept. His thoughts were of Jane and himself. What was he going to do? It wasn't fair to the girl or himself to let their emotions toward one another grow and not have an honest foundation for them to develop on. Someday he would tell her everything. He knew that. Her questions that evening under the huge old oaks down the road had come as a shock to him. What did she know about his past life? Was it a sweetheart of the past she was inquiring about or was it his connection to the federal department? Of one thing he was positive. There was no sweetheart of the past life for which he now yearned. There never had been. So try as he might to fathom her meaning of all this questioning, only one other thing was left unexplained. And that was his being a revenue man. What could she have meant?

Now more than ever came the conviction that Jane knew his secret. Another conviction came to him in the still cold hours of midnight. All things about this wonderful, beautiful, sweet, honest girl cried aloud that she loved him. Her speech, her eyes, her actions around him, the way she clung to him with fierce trembling embrace when he kissed her sweet rose-petal lips. She knew he was a federal agent and had come into this country to apprehend people who made whiskey illegally. And her father and Jim Debassius had done a lot of hard to explain, mysterious night riding since his advent into this country that was very questionable. What job could those men have that would call for such behavior? What legal job, that is? All forms of farm work was done in the daytime, and certainly they weren't working any night shift in a mine. Jane knew all this, and knowing that he had come into this country to arrest all engaged in illegal activities of liquor manufacture, had reacted only in a natural way. That, and only that, was the reason for her hesitation about committing herself completely about her emotional regard for him. Her secret fear was that eventually he might be the means of placing her father, or some close friend, behind bars. And her loyalty to her own, and their age-old customs and habits, was waging a war with her heart for supremacy in his matter.

There were times when he had seriously considered going to Lige Burton and having a man to man talk with him. But such consideration was short lived, because he had only to remember the subdued wrath of the mountaineer, and the quiet deadly mien of the Indian, that evening they had rode home, cursing revenue men during his convalescence, to know any admission of that sort would be nothing short of disastrous. Before sleep claimed him at last, he felt a premonition that someday the black-bearded giant would discover his true intention, and inwardly he quaked, for then he knew there would be hell to pay.

He was awakened next morning by Jim shaking his left shoulder which stuck out of the covers. The Indian was fully dressed. He greeted Tom in his lazy, cool way.

"Mawnin Bell, roll out now. Lige'll be over here directly poundin' on the door and rarin' to go. It's darker'en a wolf's mouth outside yet, but by the time everybody's ready to hit the trail, and have at breakfast it'll be time to haul our freights."

"Good morning Jim," Tom replied. "I'll scramble right out of bed but I sure hate to. Bet it'll be cold as the north pole up on them ridges back there. My guess is that Jane's still in bed. What time is it?"

"Quarter to five, and I contend you're wrong if you say Jane is still huggin' her piller'. Everytime we ever went huntin' before she was up bright an early an' ready to go when we was."

He strode to the door opening it and looked out and across at the main cabin. Then he swung his gaze up to the dark sky.

"Reckon we'll have a fine day for the hunt. I see stars shining' up there. Now if them there bears have been out galavantin' round last night, lookin' for a mutton chop, we'll be in luck. I'm goin' on over to the kitchen Tom, come along when you're ready." Debassius shut the door when he went out. Tom had noticed that the Indian had on a light woolen jacket, heavy shirt, high-top leather shoes, with his pants tucked into the tops of them. A red cross-bar cap was on his head. Dressed this way he could stay warm, and yet could travel fast. Heavy bulky clothing was not suited for fast travel over the rough mountain terrains, trying to keep within earshot of the dogs on the trail of bear. He had been told by these mountaineers that a bear could get up and rush when forced to. He dressed in as near a like manner as the Indian as he possibly could. Even before he opened the door to enter he could hear Jane's laughing voice bantering with Jim and her father inside. Evidently they were still trying to discourage her from accompanying them. But from the way she was laughing they were having no success. As Tom entered the kitchen door, blinking in the bright lamp light, all eyes were turned upon him.

"Mawnin' son," Burton boomed out.

"Reckon' as how you-all look a bit sleepy yet. Jane must of walked you off your legs last night. She's good at that sort of thing. Ready for the big hunt?"

"Good morning Tom," Mrs. Burton spoke from the stove, "How is your appetite this morning? I sure hope it's fine. Cause you-all will be on one dandy of a goose chase today. An' take my advice an' load up with grub now."

"Good morning Tom," Jane spoke last. She looked her old self this morning and acted it. He replied to their greetings all at one time. "Good morning everybody. I'm half asleep yet, but I'll wager that I'll wake up when that crisp air up on the ridges blows on me awhile. Jane, are you and I going to ride the mules today? Your father and Jim'll be taking the two big whites. Of course we could ride the bays. But seeing as how we're the tenderfoots at this sport perhaps we had better settle for the Jack rabbits. What do you say?"

Her parents and the Indian laughed heartily at this humorous inquiry. Jane pursed up her mouth and threw a withering look his way.

"Mr. Bell," came her spirited answer. "You-all can take your chances in one of them long-eared, hunks of mule meat if you prefer to, but please excuse me. I'll take one of the bays for my mount."

"We'll have to get off and go on foot the better part of the way," her father said. "That's the way it's always been before. I say take both of the bays. Them' mules would probably climb a tree if they scented a bear, an' they ain't broke for riding' no how yet."

"Well Jane, we ride the bays. Bossman's orders. Of course the mules would have been nice too. I'm afraid they'll feel slighted and throw a kick at me next time I take my turn at hauling prop timbers with them."

"Come and eat hunters," called out Mrs. Burton. Jane had been assisting her mother in the preparation of breakfast. She had packed a sizable lunch of sandwiches to take along on the hunt. At the breakfast call, she sat down with the men and

ate a good meal for the long tough hours ahead.

Eggs, bacon, bread and butter, and a dessert of

home canned blackberries. The three men likewise

fortified themselves against hunger and fatigue. All

three men drank two cups of hot black coffee. Jane

declined having any. The meal was eaten in almost

complete silence. The bearded giant asked

Debassius if he had the thirty-thirty ready for

business, to which he received a reply in the

affirmative.

"Feed the dogs lightly Lucy." Burton

addressed his wife. "They won't track or trail right

if they have full bellied. I'm through eatin' so think

I'll go out to the barn and saddle up my hoss'. Get

a rustle on soon as you've swallowed your grub,

folks. We want to surprise them murderin' sons at the scene of the crime if we can. Soon as it begins to get light, they'll begin to sneak back into the woods."

"Lige, are you-all goin' to pack a shootin' iron?" drawled Debassius.

"Bet your life I am. My trusty thirty-eight. That'll stop one iffin' he should get too close for comfort."

"Tom, are you carryin' a gun on this jaunt?" again inquired the Indian.

"Yes, I think I'll try and take that double barreled sixteen-gauge along just for comfort. I'll do my best to stay close to Jane, cause she'll be a walking and riding around and if any unfriendly bear comes close to me and I git' scared and miss with my two barrels, she can plug it. By the way Jane, what kind of gun are you shooting today? Something sort of heavy?"

"Oh, have no fear Tom," she laughed at him. "I'm taking along a thirty-thirty also; one of those carbine types. Dad taught me how to shoot it so I'll do my best to bring down any and all bears who are unfortunate enough to get into sights."

"Rustle along, everybody," Burton said. "I'm headin' for the barn to begin to saddle up. Git' you're shootin' irons and grub you're goin' to tote along on this hunt and dress so's you're not like you'll be in a bed tick when you-all start amblin' along on foot after them dogs. Lucy, wish us luck and don't worry. We'll do our best to keep out of the critter's reach and also try and shoot the bears an' not each other. Reckon' as how it'll be evenin' fore' we hit home again."

"Good luck all of you," Mrs. Burton replies. "Do be careful. I'll look for you-all when I see you comin'."

The mountaineer immediately quit the kitchen and headed for the barn. The dogs, Tom, Dick, and Harry, were licking their chops from their light breakfast. They clustered around the farmer's feet as he strolled along. Occasionally one of them would reach up to their master and thrust a cold damp nose in the palm of one of his hands that swung at his side. Instinctively they knew a hunt was in the offing. Their frisking and capering, and excited yips spoke more than words of their anticipation. All three of them bore scars of former close associations with bears. But if they still remembered how they had obtained those disfigurations, at the moment their actions certainly did not evidence it.

"Well, well, old boys," boomed out the bearded giant to them. "All excited and raring to go I see. Let's hope every one of you feel that frisky an' good come evenin'." They answered him with excited barking and tumbling around.

Very shortly Jim Debassius and Tom and

Jane arrived at the barn. Burton had already saddled up the big white horse which he rode. He gave Jane and Tom a hand at putting the saddles on the two bays. There were only three riding saddles to be had so the Indian gave his to Tom and clinched a folded blanket on the back of the other big white horse as a seat for him to ride upon.

"Reckon I'll do just as well with this get-up as with a saddle," he said in his laconic way. "What with the many time I'll be getin' off and on my hoss', lookin' for tracks, an' walkin' up the real steep bad places."

In a few minutes everybody was ready to ride. They swung up onto their mounts and swung off up the creek, their firearms held across their laps. Burton rode in the lead, followed by the Indian. Tom and Jane brought up the rear. The three hounds were out in front, loping long, nose to the ground, or at time the wind.

Grey daylight was just breaking over the high country when the four rode high into the immense cove where the mountaineer had seen the handiwork of the marauding animal, or animals the day before.

The day promised to be clear and brisk. A white, snow like frost covered the gray bleached out grass. Signs of the rising sun was appearing in the east. The few trees that dotted the huge cove, below the timber-line, stood out stark and bare against the lightening sky of the fall morning.

As they neared the remains of the first ewe the farmer had found, a singular change came over the dogs. A sharp eager keenness had entered their actions. They began circling about, noses hugging the ground, giving out subdued grunts of anger. Abruptly the lead dog gave an excited yelp, followed almost immediately by a long drawn-out bay. At that moment the other two dogs swung into action and all three raced away, up and up, in almost a straight line for the ridge and the edge of the timber. By their tones of voice the hunters knew they had struck a fresh trail of some animal.

"Reckon as them dogs have struck a fresh trail Jim," rolled out Burton. "What say we dismount an' see iffin' we can spot any fresh bear tracks in the frosty grass."

"Just what I was thinkin'," replied Debassius. He pulled the big white horse he was astride of to a halt and slid off its back. Bending down he cast an eagle eye upon the frosted grass in the immediate vicinity where the dogs had struck the trail. Hunched over the Indian moved about in a short circle. The eyes of the other three hunters watched him keenly. Suddenly he stopped his half-crawling motion over the grass. A low grunt of satisfaction escaped him. He pointed with a long arm at something he had found in the grass before him. Tom, Jane, and her father rode close beside the squatting Debassius. The revenue man bent a sharp eye upon the spot where the Indian was pointing. Then he saw it. There imprinted on the frosty surface of the dead grass was a large oblong mark. He swung his glance up the slope and was thrilled to his very depths by the imprints he saw. The marks on the grass were as if a man of large stature had wrapped his feet in clothes and had walked up the slope. Burton rolled a deep curse form his beard and spoke to the Indian.

"Bear tracks Jim, an' no mistake no doubt made by the old devil who killed my sheep. There might be more than one, an' I calculate there is. Come on, mount up and let's be after them dogs. By the faint sounds I hear of their barking, they must be over in that stand of virgin timber. Let's go now an' see if we can come up close to them an' what they're trailin'."

Jim rose immediately from his half-setting position on the grass and sprang upon the back of his horse. How like his hunting forefathers he looked Tom thought. With his long lean body, his sharp features, with thin high-cheek bones, his black piercing eyes with thin hawk-like sharpness. Truly at that moment the man was a red hunter.

The moment the Indian regained his seat upon his horse Burton gave a bellowing yell and sent his mount running up the slope. Debassius drove his horse ahead and in a moment or so was riding abreast of his employer.

Tom and Jane thumped their heels against their horses ribs and sent them crashing after the swift pair of whites in the lead. By the time they had reached the summit of the ridge, above where the bear, or bears, had killed the young ewes, full daylight had come.

The trees at the upper edge of the immense cove grew far enough apart to permit riding at a good pace through them.

As Burton and Debassius gained the crest of the ridge they momentarily pulled their mounts to a halt. Pausing but a moment they seemed to be listening to the trailing dogs ahead. They evidently satisfied with what they heard, they raised their right arms aloft and motioned to the fore, and down the slope to their right where the stand of big timber stood. Immediately they sent their horses in the direction they had indicated, and their ringing yells floated on the morning breeze back to Tom and Jane.

As they topped the timbered ridge they could see the two horsemen a considerable distance ahead streaking through the trees. The dogs could be heard baying for down the slope. Evidently that which they were trailing was heading down into the virgin stand of timber of which Burton spoke.

Jane and Tom drove their mounts out and down the sloping ridge in the wake of her father and the Indian. Tom permitted her to take the lead and it was a delight to him to watch the girl expertly guide her horse through the trees and still maintain a goodly rate of speed. Occasionally she would glance back over her shoulder at him and waving an arm aloft peal out an exultant Tomboyish yell. How keenly she seemed to be enjoying this brisk exhilarating ride. As she looked at him and gave her a ringing yell, he would grin and wave and yell in reply. Conversation was out of the question while they raced along at this ground-covering pace.

The second growth of young timber on this side of the ridge began to grow more thickly. Riding became more difficult, what with the tangled patches of underbrush, the old rotting stumps and logs which stood and lay, about in all directions. In some places they were forced to slow their mounts to a walk.

After a few minutes of this tough going Jane yelled back at Tom that the big trees were just ahead. She was trailing her father and the Indian who by this time was out of sight ahead. Occasionally their far off yells could be heard. Tom wondered how close to the dogs they were. From what the mountaineer and Debassius had said they expected the bears to swing down this slope and eventually turn to their left and again climb another slope on the opposite side of the stand of big timber and make for the laurel beds on the top of the far ridge.

Tom noticed, almost immediately after Jane had yelled back to him that the stand of big trees were just ahead, a lessening of the obstructions to their travel. The young trees were thinning out again.

Almost without warning he burst from amongst the smaller, younger timber into the midst of trees that had seen the storms of centuries roll over their lofty heads. The only warning he received of their sudden change was a sharp sudden falling away of the trees of smaller, shorter stature only to be replaced by lofty giants, whose round straight trunks climbed and climbed into the pink streaked heavens. As the revenue man rode along in the rear of the fast traveling girl he could see trees standing on every hand of huge sizes. He remembered the old rotting stumps he had run into before all along the roadside on his journey into this mountain country, and now knew that those huge old stumps had once held trees like this magnificent stand of timber. He loved big tall straight timber, and looking at this beautiful stand of forest monarchs understood the mountaineers' reluctance to out this virgin tract.

Here under the big trees travel was considerable improved. Jane rode on at what Tom considered a break neck speed. Her pealing cries floated back to him as she flashed swiftly on among the stately monarchs. Throwing caution to the winds he urged his mount to greater effort.

The ride down the virgin timbered slope to the ravine below was a thrilling one for the revenue man. It was something the likes of which he had never experienced before. The horse he rode seemed to have contracted the contagious feeling of excitement. Clamping the bit firmly between his iron jaws he plowed on down the mountain side, at times slipping and sliding wildly down steep descents, sending the dry boughs and loose leaf mold flying in all directions from his shod hooves. At other times crashing recklessly through stands of underbrush that almost whipped his rider from the saddle. Or then again he would break the trunk of one of the huge trees so violently that if Tom hadn't been intently watching his path of progress he might have suffered a broken leg. Vainly he tried talking his mount into a calmer state but the powerfully muscled bay heeded him not. He ran recklessly on, determined to close the gap, if possible, which separated him from the three horses ahead. Disregarding all thought of dignified horsemanship, Tom clutched the saddle horn with his left hand, having thrust the double barreled shotgun he carried under that arm and hugging it to his side. His right hand held the reins, but for all attention the bay paid the pressure he put upon them he might as well have been holding a couple of twine strings. Jane had disappeared somewhere ahead. Her thrilling cries still rang out but faintly. At the pace she was driving her horse through the timber Tom expected any moment to come across her lying senseless on the ground, where she had been violently knocked from her saddle because her horse had run headlong into a tree. He crashed on, but his fears for the girl he loved did not materialize. The leaf covered floor of the forest through which he rode was void of crumpled human form.

Abruptly he came to the edge of the stand of virgin timber. Here again the going was through trees of miniature size compared to the ones immediately to the rear. The stand of big trees swung off at right angles in the direction he was traveling and the tall straight trunks marched away into the distance.

How far it was down that mountain slope to the ravine below the revenue man had not the faintest idea. He knew he had rode a considerable distance. When at last he rode his skidding mount down the steep grade into the ravine, he was surprised and delighted to find Jane waiting for him. The big bay horse she was astride came to a crawling, heaving halt, the instant it regained the side of the bay Jane was riding. She laughed aloud.

At the undignified picture Tom presented as he rode down the steep grade. He was riding reared back in the saddle as if he feared falling over the horses head. And his fears might well be justified, because descending this sharp ascent the big bays haunches was considerably higher than his front quarters. Thus throwing his rider forward in a most uncomfortable manner. Burton and the Indian was nowhere in sight.

"Howdy slow poke," she greeted him gaily. "Was you-all taking a peaceful little canter through the woods?"

"Jane Burton, I honestly never took such a wild ride in my life," he answered her serious faced. "This jug head of a horse wouldn't listen to a thing I said to him. Every minute on that mad dash from the top of the ridge back there I expected to be knocked out of the saddle, and I say it's a miracle I wasn't. Where's your father and Jim? And are you-all in one piece?"

"Sure Mr. Bell. I'm in one place," she told him with a wide grim upon her pretty face. "Pardon me, but looks to me like I should of begged and even insisted that you-all stay home. As I recall you-all was the one who so vigorously tried to persuade a girl I know to remain behind – out of harm's way. Am I right, Mr. Tom?"

"Alright, alright, you reckless tomboy rub it in," he told her red faced. "But I still say this sort of thing is not for a girl. Even though I am now positive you'll never agree with me."

"When I got down to the creek here, Daddy and Jim was just starting up that slope you-all can see over there and ahead. They yelled and waved at me an' pointed up ahead. The way I figure it that's the way the bear is headin', an' beck there on top of that high ridge in the big laurel thicket Daddy spoke of."

Bell looked then at the creek. It was about three or four yards wide and was rushing along between timbered banks. All along its entire length he could see the stream seemed to be one continuous riffle, dashing merrily on its way over, and among rocks of varying size. The water of this woods brook was a crystal ember. Nowhere did it look to be more than knee deep to their horses.

"Jane, honey, forgive my serious face of a moment ago," Tom said to her. "You know I am always thinking of you and of your wellbeing. Is this still your father's land?"

"No, daddy's land ended back there at the edge of the big trees. It runs south and west a good ways off in that direction up there. How did you like the looks of that virgin stand?"

"I loved those big fellows Jane. I would liked to have seen this country before any of the timber was out. Sure would have been a sight worth seeing. Do you like big old trees?"

"My land yes," instantly came her reply.

"Since I've been big enough to appreciate things that have endured for years and years. Maybe my regard for that block of magnificent timber has sort of stayed Daddy's hands about selling it. He could realize a considerable hunk of money if he would see that old matured stand, but I hope he never does. Now about this land right here. It used to belong to a big timber company back east. They cut, or butchered, the timber off it years ago and then turned the land back to the government. Daddy says these mountains that are all covered with woods for miles and miles, will someday be made into a national forest."

"Honey, don't you think we had better be moving along? If we don't come up with your father and Jim soon they'll have the bear shot and skinned out and will meet us coming back."

"No, they won't." She stoutly said, "They both promised me this morning, before you came into the kitchen, that there'd be no shooting of any bears before you and I came up to where the dogs had them tread. Yes, let's go. We'll ride up that slope ahead and across the creek. I won't guarantee how far we'll be able to ride the horses, but we'll go as far as we can, an' then walk the rest of the way to where the action begins. Let's take it easy up the other side of this mountain. That way it'll be easier on both the horses and their riders."

"O.K. I'll slow down." She laughed out, "I forgot we have a slow poke in this huntin' party."

"That's all right," Tom defended his lack of enthusiasm concerning speed over this deceiving terrain. "I'd rather take it a little slower than wound up with a broken arm or leg, to say nothing of maybe a broken neck."

"That's the thrill of the chase Tom." She explained to him, "If you-all could just go out and canter up to an old fat bear and knock him in the head with a club, - well, I ask you – what sport would that be. This way you know you're trailin' a good sized animal that is wild and who would tear you to pieces if you was to get in the way. And when you finally come up to him you know you've been taken for a good long chase and when at last you shoot this bear you've got that feeling of satisfaction that you really earned all this and not merely done the shooting to pass the time away."

"I see what you mean. But I wasn't raised to all this like you was, and I'm sorry I wasn't. A background of life like this mountain country can give a person is something worthwhile to look back on in later years."

"Glad you-all think so," she said, and turning her horse at right angles urged him down the bank and into the rushing stream. Tom did likewise. He was much surprised to see how deep the crystal clear water of the stream really was. It was almost up to his horses belly and once in the middle of this deceptive brook was amazed at its swiftness. The big bay plunged along through the rushing water in the wake of the horse Jane rode, sending the icy water flying in sheets. The revenue man was glad indeed when they clambered up the opposite bank.

On the creek bank were the marks of where Burton and Debassius' mounts had climbed out of the creek. Their trail led straight away up the slope. Jane gave another of her strange thrilling cries and forged ahead of Tom up the steadily climbing mountain side. The formation of the land on this side of the creek was noticeably different from what it had been on the side they had recently descended. Ledges began to come into view. The mountain side was more bulging and the gentle slope of the opposite side was not in evidence. The trail of the bearded mountaineer and his Indian companion let straight on up.

Patches of mountain laurel began to put in their appearances. The second growth timber was more choked with underbrush. Some of this underbrush was about shoulder high to the bay Tom rode and when its' branches raked across his legs he was aware of sharp sticking sensations. Once Jane drew her mount to a halt and sat listening for sounds of her father and Jim and the dogs. Urging his mount up near hers he also stopped. They were at the top of one of the ledges below. Far ahead and lots higher then where they were listening they could hear the hounds barking. How faint and far away the sounds were. Tom wondered if the dogs were at the big laurel thicket. Or if they had forged their quarry up a tree before the laurel thicket was reached. Close beside their heaving horses he noticed another clump of the underbrush with the sharp stickers. Calling Jane's attention to it he inquired of her if she knew what it was.

"Oh, that small bunch of bushes with all those stickers on it?" She said, waving a hand at the bushes indicated. "That's prickly ash, an' it sure can stick you. Daddy says it's good for a number of things. Made into medicine I mean. People here about boil the bark of that mean sticky little bush and make a tea of it. Old folks says it's good to ward off havin' a stroke. The stuff they cook up from the bark sure is bitter. About the name it's yellow-root tea." And she wrinkled her small pretty nose up at the memory of this unpleasant homemade remedy.

"That's one sticky little tree and no mistake," Tom agreed. "Well I say let's be on our way. Our horses have got their breath from the steep climbing we have done since crossing the creek. We can hear the dogs up ahead, maybe they've treed something and your father and Jim are waiting for us to get there. Hard telling how much farther we can ride the horses. I've been near swiped out of the saddle several times and so far and I must say it would have been more comfortable over this brushy, steep, ledgy land to have walked."

"I'm going to ride this nag I'm on far as it can take me," Jane stated. "That walking up this steep mountain is not what it's cracked up to be.

Well, let's be on our way, and my huntin'

companion please keep up." And tossing her chin

in the air, and giving him a raised eyebrow look

the rosy cheeked girl clucked to her horse and

again resumed the trailing of the father and the

Indian up the bulging mountainside.

Up and up they climbed, and always the

landscape was of the rocky uneven type. At times

the growth of young timbers almost failed, only to

be replaced by immense patches of blackberry

vines, interspersed with the ever increasing

presence of mountain laurel. Eventually, after

much strenuous climbing on the part of the horses

they pushed up over a jutting shoulder onto more

gentle sloping land. The sounds of the barking

dogs came from directly ahead. The growth of young trees was more prominent on this gentle slope. Intermingled with the young trees was an occasional old gnarled birch. Some of these hardwood trees were as much as three feet in diameter at the butt, indicating in an undisputable way their old age. None of these unmovable birches were fit for lumber, which probably accounted for them still standing.

Jane gave another of her strangely thrilling cries and urged her mount ahead, and up the lope through the trees. The trail her father and Debassius had left was very plain to see. Tom yelled out lustily and tried to get some semblance of speed from his tiring mount. The horse responded as best he could and went loping ahead up the grade. Suddenly a ringing yell fell upon his ears. Looking directly ahead and a little to the left he spied the Indian sitting his big white horse, which was standing on top of a large flat rock. Again the Indian gave his stentorian cry and with long arm waved to the approaching riders. Burton sat his horse in the background. Jane and Tom both yelled in reply and raced on to where her father and Jim were waiting. Burton greeted them in his booming voice, but the Indian merely smiled in his slow, lazy, easy way.

"Well, well, see you-all finally made that trek up the mountain," he greeted them, and laughed deep in his beard. "Howsoever, your hosses' carried you-all an' so maybe it wasn't too rough. Pears' to me that the two of you does look a little done-in at that." "Daddy please don't keep us in suspense any longer," Jane implored. "Them dogs are barkin' right close to us here, Do they have a bear tread?"

"Shore' it didn't look like a ground hog to me that was pushed up in that tree out there, when I slipped up and took a peak a while ago." And the usual reticent red man gave a low chuckle when he delivered this bit of information.

"Is it a good sized bear that the dogs have treed?" Tom inquired.

"Jim says it looks to him like it is an old male that is roostin' up there on a big limb," informed the mountaineer. "We'll leave all four of our hosses' right here, and take my advice to tie them tight. They would shore' jump out of their skins if we was to ride them up to the tree where the bear is."

"Don't be any disappointed if that bear takes off when he sees us comin'," said Debassius. "My guess is that we'll have to have the dogs rout 'em out of that laurel thicket before we're thorough."

"Oh, I'm so excited," Jane cried out, and slid out of her saddle. "I'll probably be scared stiff when that old boy is right before me."

"Maybe you'd better stay here with the horses," Tom offered, and knew she would jump down his throat at such an idea.

"How does the idea strike you Jane girl?" her father smiling inquired of her.

"Perfectly rotten," she grimaced. "However I thank Tom very kindly for his consideration of me."

"Well since you're not going to be with us," Jim laughed, "I suggest we push along, an' introduce ourselves to the boy in the trees." Jane laughed out in her musical way and hurriedly dismounting tied her horse to a young birch and taking her carbine started towards where the dogs were raising their voices. The three men grinned at her and processed to follow suit. Each carried a gun ready for action.

About five hundred feet separated them from where the dogs were barking treed. The sun was shining brightly down through the young timber, and each tree was distinctly seen for a considerable distance on all sides. There were no leaves on their branches to obstruct ones' view.

A moments walking and the dogs were seen jumping around the butt of a beech. Upon nearer observation the trees were seen to be one of about fifteen inches or so in diameter at the butt. Limbs grew on this tree to within about five feet of the ground.

As they cautiously advanced Tom scanned it up and down freely. Some bleached out leaves still clung to the branches of this specimen. At first he saw nothing in the tree. Then suddenly his heart gave a great leap. A blackish something, of considerable size, was to be seen about half way up. Watching it closely he saw it move. Slowly the dark thing in the tree was descending. As it came closer and closer to the ground the dogs frenzied in their leaping into the air and barking.

When Burton and the Indian saw the descending black mass in the beech they yelled loudly and started to run forward. When they were within a hundred feet of the dogs, a huge round black ball of fur dropped out of the lower limbs of the trees squarely into the midst of the hounds.

At the instant this happened, bedlam broke

loose with snarls of rage the three dogs pounced upon this big round ball of black fur. A roar burst from that ball of fur. Instantly it was transformed into a savage, snarling, striking, biting fury. It was then that it took distinct shape. Out of that mass of snarling dogs rose a huge black form that stood upright like a man, with great swinging head, and slavering jaws, and huge black paws that shot out and amid the onslaught of the enraged canines with the speed, and skill of a trained boxer. What amazing power lurked in those lightning swift paws. What destructive ability they seemed to possess. One dog was knocked kicking in an instant, another was clasped to that barrel-like hairy chest and severely bitten, and with one swipe of a paw the third dog was sent end-over-end.

When the huge black animal reared up from the ground near the besieging dogs Tom was thrilled to his toes. It was a big black bear he was gazing bug-eyed at, and it needed only one glance to see that the huge animal was fighting mad. Coughing roars and grunts came from its gasping jaws, its little pig-like eyes were possessed of a fateful glare. It was the light of battle, swinging its great head round and it sent a snarling roar at the four humans who were close by. Tom stood rooted to the spot. He glanced at Jane and was electrified. She was burying a cartridge into the chamber of her high-powered rifle.

A piercing cry rose above the sounds of the battling bear and dogs. Throwing a quick glance to his right, Tom spied the Indian standing in a singular way. His lean raven haired head was thrust forward like the head of a bird of prey. His thirty-thirty rifle was half way to his shoulder. Again he gave his piercing gaze. The bear swung round to face the sound of that cry and in swinging dropped to all fours. For an instant the enraged bear glared at the red hunter. Simultaneously, a sharp whip-like crack sounded, instantly followed by a dull thumping sound. The bear snapped at something that bit into his left shoulder. A roar of rage came from its hairy throat. Then turning round it retreated into the underbrush leaving a crimson trial behind. The dogs painfully took up the task of again tracking down their ferocious quarry. However the dog called Dick made no more to resume the trail. He was the one of the three who had been bitten and evidently wanted no further association with the bear for the present. He lay exhausted where the big mauler had thrown him. Jane ran to Dick's side and bent down to see how badly he was injured. Gently she began to explore his wounds. Burton and Debassius instantly gave chase to the fleeing bruin, guns ready for lightning swift use.

"Jane, let's get after that bear," said Tom running over to where she was kneeling beside the injured dog.

"O. K. but first let me see if I can help Dick to be more comfortable till we come back this way on our way home. He's not hurt bad, far as I can see, but just played out. Of course, that terrible bear hit him a lot, but he'll get over it."

"What a demon that big black devil was," Tom told her breathlessly. "I know now what you meant when you said it takes effort and risk to conquer a wild beast like that. Those poor sheep never had a chance against him"

"Us people of this mountain country have lots of things to fight, in order that we might survive. And not all of them things are four footed," she said significantly. Tom wondered at her hidden meaning. In all probability she might be referring to him and others of like profession. But the present was no time to worry about such as that. He wanted very much to be in at the finish when that black fighting fury was made to bite the dust.

"I'm going Jane," he told her. "I want to be present when that sheep killer gets his."

"I'm right behind you," she answered him. "I also want to witness that little event myself," giving the injured dog a last affectionate pet on his sagging head. She rose from her kneeling position, and taking up the carbine hurried after the fast walking revenue man.

The dogs ahead were barking ahead again, and they could hear Burton and Debassius yelling. Making as fast progress as they could they soon came to the vicinity where the sounds of strife were coming from. The big black bear hadn't made the refuge of the laurel bed. He had been brought

126

to bay against a cluster of boulders of various sizes. Some of the rocks were big as a hay stack while others were of more diminutive size. As Tom and Jane rushed up to where her father and the Indian were standing they spotted the bear standing up with its back against one of the largest boulders. The dogs were circling around in front of the trapped animal, barking the while. However, they were maintaining a respectful distance.

The Indian was angling for a heart shot. He was approaching close to where the beleagured animal was facing its hecklers. Sharp eyes darting from side to side, its great head swinging to end from the while. Occasionally the wounded beast would drop to all fours and advance a step or two, at which time the remaining two legs would drop quietly back out of reach of those deadly paws.

"Drop him Jim," Burton kept yelling at the Indian, "or he'll kill them two hounds yet."

Debassius answered not a word, but kept up his singular advance. At last he was within fifty feet of the bear and standing behind a squarish boulder of about three feet in height and approximately the same width. Kneeling behind this protection he thrust his high-powered rifle across its seemed top. Watching the Indian Tom surmised that he had chosen this protective position with the thought in mind that if the bear charged when he shot he would have something between himself and the furry ball of destruction.

Scarcely had Debassius bulwarked himself when the huge black bear again rose upright to a standing position. He roared forth his challenge to dog and man alike. Looking at the frightful bloody beast the revenue man could but admire the besieged monarch of the high country. He sallied forth from his lair on raids whenever the urge possessed him, asking permission from nobody. But like the bold pirate who raided on the high seas, in days gone by, his days of reparation had come. And he was meeting his enemies with a matchless courage and raging fury. There was none of the craven in this old raider of the hills.

When the big bear lifted himself from all fours to his standing position the watching and waiting Indian also moved. Dropping his cheek to the stock of the powerful Winchester, he took careful aim at the broad hairy chest fifty feet away.

The angry monarch sent forth again his challenging roar, and swung in a direct line with the waiting rifleman. A ringing whip-like report sounded above the commotion made by the hunted and the hunter. A dull thudding sound instantly followed the report. The huge bear swinging fore paws dropped to his sides at the sound of the rifle, and he swayed on his hind legs unsteadily. A moment more and he crashed to the earth. Instantly the two hounds pounced upon him, only to be just as quickly knocked end over end. Up from the leaf covered soil reared the mighty beast and coughing and roaring out his lifes' blood charged for the squarish rock, behind which crouched the Indian.

The swiftly advancing bear was a sight to chill ones blood, but Debassius with a wild yell sprang to his feet and leveling the rifle at the onrushing destruction sent shot after shot into the body of the huge black beast.

Four shots rang out before the ferocious animal was brought to a crashing stop. In the space of time while the Indian was working his rifle lever and firing the gun, the bear had charged to within a half dozen yards of his miniature Gibraltar. After the beast had fallen under the stress of lead, the dogs were permitted to worry the lifeless carcass for a while before either the mountaineer or his Indian employee would approach it.

"Well it's all over for another bear," Jane cried out rushing closer to stand beside her father and Jim. Tom walked over to within a dozen feet of the fallen monarch, expecting even now to see it charge up from where it lay sprawled loosely on the leaves, and have everything and everybody flee before it.

A moment more and Jim stepped to the lifeless body. Whipping out his eight inch hunting knife, he straightaway began skinning out the big beast. Burton strode to his side and prepared to assist him. Together they turned the heavy body on its back, then grasping a huge claw tipped fore paw the Indian inserted the keen blade of his knife just under the furry hide and pushed downward with the keen blade toward the belly of the animal. By holding his knife at this angel he was able to split

open the hide inside the foreleg down to a point

between the forelegs. The other front leg was

treated in similar fashion. Then walking to the rear

of the carcass he proceeded on the front ones. After

the hide of all four legs had been split in this

fashion a different operation came into use.

Inserting the sharp edge of his blade in the skin

between the hind legs, where the two inside slits

met he pushed the blade straight up the center of

the belly of the carcass clear up to the edge of the

lower jaw. Then each man fell to skinning out the

bear. Debassius at one end, Burton at the other.

The mountaineer produced a long clasp knife with

a five inch blade to do his skinning with. Swiftly

the furry hide was peeled down the legs, and along

each side of the cut Debassius had made up the

belly. Jane turned away from the gruesome work. The dogs lolled around, watching with avid eyes, the while licking the marks of battle the bear had inflicted upon their bodies.

"Daddy while you an' Jim are skinnin' out this old monster I think I'll take Tom out the ridge here aways an' show him the big laurel bed where the bears hide sometimes. Do you care if I do?" As Jane made her request her father looked up at her, and grinning laughed aloud in his booming way. Debassius gave a low chuckle.

"Go ahead Janie girl," the big man laughed. "Don't reckon this is any sight to please a lady no how. Be careful you two an' don't run afoul of any bears on the prod. That big bed of laurel is home to more of them brutes than this one here. Be back in about an hour, as Jim an' I we'll be through here an' ready to hit the trail home."

"We'll be careful Mr. Burton," Tom told him. "I'll see that Jane has her carbine along."

They started out the wild, lonely ridge, the girl tripping lightly along in the lead. Tom carried the rifle. To each side of where they tread, the second growth forest stretched away in unbroken formation. The fall air was keen and sharp in their faces. While foamy clouds had begun to push up in the western sky with darker hue on their undersides. Looking at the clouds Jane turned and smiled at the man walking in the rear.

"It looks like snow clouds in the sky off there to the northwest Tom," She stated, "An' I for one wouldn't be at all surprised if we get up most any morning now an' find some on the ground."

"Do you like snow, little girl?" he inquired.

"Tom, guess I do, But I used to like it more than I do now. But that's the way with everybody they tell me. What you like as a kid, you don't care for when you grow older. Do you like it?"

"My experience with snow has been much the same as yours. Then I did and now I am not so enthusiastic about the fluffy white stuff."

"I like snow for Christmas though," she said

dropping back to where he was walking to take him by the hand. She looked up into his face a few inches above her own. He smiled down at the flushed face of this mountain rose. "Are you-all goin' to get me something pretty for Christmas when it rolls around?"

"Of course I am," he replied. "I have already given you the best I could give any girl. I'm speaking of my heart, you big eyed girl of my dreams. But then I'll get you another present or two to go with the first one I mentioned."

Tightening his fingers around the small hand that nestled in his right one, he came to a halt. How big and expressive the brown eyes raised to his in that moment. How intent and mysterious their gaze. How irresistible the sweet parted lips, the rosy-cheeked oval face, with its frame of brilliant brownish copper tinted hair. She devised his thought as he gazed down upon her. His other arm swung round her shoulders to clasp her in an eager embrace. He bent his head to her upturned face, and kissed her again and again.

"I've been aching to hug and kiss you all this day. And you darling, cute, rosy cheeked little minx if I didn't love you so awful much I'd eat you up! Right here and now."

"Do you really love me, Tom?" she asked him serious faced.

"On my word of honor I love you. I feel

about you as I've never felt about any girl before in my life." Flinging her arms around him the girl hugged him tightly. A few more moments they stood in close embrace. Once more kisses were exchanged, then they started on out the timbered ridge.

Soon he could see a tangled mass of green ahead through the trees. Jane spoke up telling him that the huge laurel thicket was directly ahead. As they came to the edge of the evergreen bed, an interesting sight met him. A tangled copse of bush-like growth covered several acres. This evergreen shrubbery was of goodly size directly to the fore was those growing, whose trunks were thick as a grown man's body at their base. Immediately upon rising from the surface of the soil they split or divided into numerous scaly green trunks, the largest of which were no larger than a man's arm. This was not the smaller mountain laurel, but of the type known as rhododendron, or giant mountain laurel. Some of the trunks of this evergreen rose to a height of more than a dozen feet. And the branches of the scaly green trunks were clothed with long dark green fan-like leaves, some of which were more than eight inches in length and close to three in width. This foliage was heavy and thick upon examination. The huge bed of laurel was growing and intergrowing. The long thin trunks evidently grew so tall that they were forced down to the ground by their top heavy condition. And Tom noticed that where the slim green trunks had bent over in this fashion where they touched the ground that part of the trunk had taken root again. This formed a huge knuckle that stuck up, and it was noticeable that the undergrowth of the big laurel bed was a tangled confusion of loops and knuckles. The evergreen leaves of this annoying bush were such a dense copse that the revenue man doubted if much snow ever reached to the bottom of the bed. He decided to ask Jane about this.

"Honey, this is some sight," he told her. "I saw plenty of laurel on my trip up through this mountain country, but never did I see anything to equal this. From looking at that green leafy tangled mass before us I'd say the snow doesn't often reach to the ground under that bed. How about it?"

"Jim says it seldom does," she replied,

snuggling up close to his side. "He had been out on this ridge in winter when there was a deep snow on an he always said bears had a warm dry place to hibernate in, under all this twisted, tangled laurel thicket. Notice there are some places back under there that looks just like big round black holes. That old fellow we got today was sure tryin' to make it to his place. But he didn't."

"How big a patch of this evergreen shrub is there in this bed?"

"Daddy and Jim both say there's well onto ten acres. However, that's hard to say for sure."

"Here is a wilderness. So wild looking. Looks like pictures of places in the jungle tropics

I've seen."

"All this beautiful mountain country is a mysterious wilderness Tom." Jane said in low tones, flinging out an arm and pointing first this way, and then that way. "But we'd better be headin' back to where Daddy and Jim are at. They'll be out here looking for us soon." Looking up into his face she asked him a question in the straightforward way she had. "Do you-all like my mountains, Tom?"

"I love every square foot of this big rough, lonely, high country. Love its wild miles and miles of endless forest. Love its high altitudes, its lonely dark forbidding face, its rushing crystal streams and rivers, and I guess most of all I love the down to earth, homely, God fearing people who populate it. And right this minute a girl of this mountain country is standing by my side who I love, and love, and love."

"Thanks for all the nice things you-all just said," she whispered, and raising on tip toe kissed him squarely on the mouth, "May there never be anything happen that would change your opinion of this country an' its' people."

He took her again in his arms. Her quiet somber mood with all its tenderness impressed him to pour out his heart to her. Tell her everything and have done with this deception. But some strange indefinable thing stayed his tongue. He felt he must play his double role for yet a little while. Of late he had entertained the thought of going and having a man to man, heart to heart, talk with old preacher Kane. There was a something about that man Kane that inspired him to take the old philosopher of life into his confidence. But not just yet.

"Don't look so down hearted, Jane girl. The only thing that could sour me on this country is for you to turn against me, give me the cold shoulder and never let me take you in my arms again or kiss you, or be kissed by you. Never have you hold my hand or speak lovingly to me anymore. Know what I mean?"

Quickly she nodded her head and pulling his face down to hers kissed him three times, hard and passionately.

"Does that make you-all feel any better now?" she inquired of him.

"I feel like flying back to the house now instead of having to ride that big devil of a bay, and I feel like picking you up and taking you along on my flight."

At his words Jane disengaged herself from his embrace and smiling up at him, she took his arm and started back the way they had come from where her father and the Indian was skinning out the big black bear.

When they arrived at the scene of the last

fight the old bear had put up, they found Burton and Debassius ready to travel, and waiting for them. The hide had been stripped from the carcass of the big brute.

They had cut a section out of one of the hind legs, close up to where it joined the body. The hide was rolled up into a furry ball. The big man with the beard greeted them with his usual booming way. Pointing at the bear skin he gave a low laugh.

"Reckon' as how the pelt of that old robber'll make a nice rug for the livin' room. Jim an' me cut out a fair bunch of steaks from that right hindleg, an' have 'em wrapped up in the hide there."

"How did you-all like that big laurel bed Tom?" drawled Debassius in his cool, easy way.

"That sure is a tangled mass of growth and regrowth," Bell answered.

"Looks to be so thick that it's doubtful if more would get down to the ground, what with all those big green leaves. Jane says bears stay under that thick growth all winter."

"I've been over to that big bed in winter when a heavy snow had crusted," said the Indian. "An' I seen bear tracks in the snow round that laurel patch on all sides. Bears come out in winter sometimes on warm days. They had big holes all back under that dense growth. Looked like a big snow covered brush pile where the rabbits had been playin' round it."

"Tell Tom about that when we get home Jim," burst out Burton. "I'm getting caved in round the middle, an' need some wet packin'. That grub Jane packed is back on her hoss', but I'll lay you odds its scrambled after the wild ride it took this morning'. Anyway I never did go for cold grub no how. Come on everybody and let's make tracks."

Catching the furry roll of hide and steaks up in his arms he took off back down the gently sloping ridge the way they had come up. Debassius strode silently at his heels. Tom and Jane, as usual, brought up the rear. The three dogs trotted along by their sides. The dog that was mauled the worst seemed to have found new strength. He kept up with the other two without difficulty. Each of the three hounds had had a rough day. They had been knocked around by the old bear something scandalous. But with rest and good food they would be ready in a few days to perform the same hunt over again.

Presently the horses were reached. When Burton tried to mount his horse with the big bear skin in his arms, the horse shied and reared up. He stomped his shod hooves and rolled his eyes. The animal could smell the bear. The hide gave off the same odor off its owner as it did while it was being worn by the big black fighter. The mountain man gave a thundering curse and brought the horse down with an iron hand and arm. The frightened animal stood quivering in every muscle. First the big man lay the bear skin down on the leaves and mounted his horse. Then he instructed Debassius to hand him the hide. The horse flattened its ears when the folded hide was laid in front of the saddle, but this time didn't try to bolt.

Soon everyone was in the saddle, and the long ridge back to the barn at home was begun. Burton and his Indian companion traveled at a much more reasonable pace going back home than what they had traveled at that morning.

Most two hours later they pulled up in the barn yards at home. All had returned safe and sound. The hunt had been a success. Everybody was tired but happy. Mrs. Burton came bustling out of the house to greet their homecoming. When her husband held up the roll of bear skin and gave his roar of greeting, the good woman smiled and nodded her head. Jane squealed out at her mother and glancing at Tom told her that when he saw the big black bear close up he up and ran like a scared rabbit. Her father roared with laughter, and Debassius gave his low chuckle. Tom looked red faced at the good woman standing smiling at the group. Jane's musical laugh sang out.

That evening at the supper table, Mrs. Burton had to hear all the details of the hunt, and the returned hunters joyfully supplied her with the information she sought. Bear steaks were upon the bill of fare for that meal. Everyone had a generous helping of the sweet port like meat. For the revenue man it was his first experience at eating that particular kind of wild meat. But he found it delicious.

The night shadows had long since fallen when he repaired to his bed in the two room cabin. The Indian had built a fire in the big open fireplace. How bright and merry the fire threw out. Far up on the ridge above the Burton home an owl hooted his mournful lonely cry. His thought drifted to the mountaineer and the Indian. Of late they had done no night riding. And it was noticeable that Mrs. Burton and Jane had seemed to have lost that occasional preoccupied look they had sometimes wore when he and the Indian had been gone so much till the wee hours in the morning. He wondered what they were engaged in to call for such hours as that. Before falling to sleep he let his mind dwell on Jane. But now, thoughts of her filled his every waking hour. How sweet and sad and mysterious she had been that day. But also how responsive to his embraces, his lips, his every endearing word spoken to her. Some day that wonderful girl will know all about me, he promised himself. He sometimes believed she already knew. He was convinced that she loved him, as he loved her. And he felt that someday she would walk by his side as his wife. Winter now was close upon the high country, and when the spring time rolled around again, what would Jane say when he asked her if she loved him. When sleep claimed him that was the thought that predominated his dreams. A brown eyed and brown haired girl who clung to him in fond embrace.

October passed in a blaze of glory. On Halloween night of that colorful month there was a dance down at the little village of Mingo in the schoolhouse. All the Burton household attended. Old preacher Kane was present, and so was Dr. and Mrs. Adams. Some of the dancers wore masquerade costumes, but mostly they came from far and wide as their natural selves.

Jane wore a small black mask across her lovely brown eyes. And Tom declared to himself she was easily the prettiest girl there. Things went smoothly except for one fight that was waged over a dispute about who was to have a certain dance with one of the Valley Head girls. The contestants looked to the revenue man to be more or less intoxicated. He overheard an interesting remark preacher Kane made to Burton concerning the fight. "Well Lige, the boys were tippin' a jug of dew out back a little too frequent. An old hard feeling and bad blood between them two made itself known. Reckon they'll cool off soon as they sober up. Howsoever, down in the Big Smokies where you an' me first saw the light of day things weren't quite so tame like as they are now. In them days many a drop of blood was shed over a good lookin' woman." The loquacious old minister had spoken in his usual soft easy way, but there had been a world of meaning in his gentle quiet tones.

Tom and Jim danced several times with Jane and other fellows out in from time to time. The girl was obviously enjoying the attention she was receiving very much. As the fiddlers played their quaint style of violin music one could not but be impressed by its beauty and infectious nature. These men of the mountains could surely pull a mean bow the revenue man confessed to himself. Some of the waltzes were played in a sobbing mournful way that seemed to cast a dreamy spell over the dancers. While the quadrilles and two-steps were played in an entirely different style. How the violins were laughing, and chuckling, the while they were singing a beautiful song. Four men played violins. They set upon that raised part of the schoolhouse floor round, and behind the teacher's desk. These men played as one. Every movement of their bows were the same, their timing was flawless. If there was any difference in their music as individuals Tom couldn't detect it. Half the time their eyes were closed as they seemed to perform miracles upon their violins. He had heard other country fiddlers' play before, but never nothing like this elderly quartet. Their music was superb, in a class by itself.

It was past midnight when the dance broke up. Except for the one fight it had been a big success. It bred goodwill and neighborliness among the people of the high country. The kindly old theologians face had a worn smile seeing his people mingling together and having a good time. Tom observed the old fellow dancing in more than one of the quadrilles. He had even danced with Jane, cutting Jim Debassius and the revenue man out with a hearty laugh and a gay smile. At the close of the merry making the people present

called upon their minister to give a prayer of

thanksgiving for their privilege of assembling

together and having a joyful time. His prayer was

short and full of meaning. Every word the elderly

minister uttered in the prayer was just right for the

occasion. Almost, it was a benediction.

The Burton family had gone to the dance in

the spring wagon, and wrapped up with heavy

quilts and blankets didn't seem to mind in the least

the frosty night air as they rode home. In the

darkness, Jane slipped her small cool hand under

the quilt she and Tom had over their laps and legs,

and clasped his hand tightly in hers. At the dance

Tom could not but notice how her big brown eyes

had flashed when he had danced with some other

girl. How eloquent her unconscious assumption of possession. Her actions spoke more clearly and loudly than shouted words that she loved him. But after home was arrived at and he was in bed, her actions, were a complete mystery to him. She was reluctant to commit herself on how she felt about him, but when other females showed up on the scene he then watched her immediate reaction. In their sweet fathomless way the opposite sex was a complete mystery to him. But then he believed he had read somewhere that no man, regardless of who he was in the past, or what he might be in the future, could understand a woman.

Next morning it was raining a cold steady rain. It wasn't a real down pour nor was it a mere drizzle either. For close to a week the cold rain descended. By the time the skies had cleared

November was nearly a week old. The second

week of November snow began to put in its

appearance on the high ridges. It fell mostly during

the night, coming down noiselessly and softly, as if

the heavens were playing a white fluffy game with

the people of this earth. The big flakes came softly

tumbling down. But what snow fell during the

night nearly always melted off the ground in the

coves and down the valleys by the time night had

come again when more might fall. By this time all

leaves had been stripped from the trees, and the

keen edge of winter began to be felt in the air.

During the time since the bear hunt Tom and Jim

had been cutting props every day the weather

would permit.

The mountain farmer had established a market for all his props, provided he would deliver them on the main road down by Mingo. So, consequently, while Tom and the Indian cut and split and picked up the props in long piles, Burton daily hauled them down to the main road.

Here heavy trucks, with solid rubber tires, hauled them away to the mines, while some were loaded in box-cars on the rail road then, and thence to their destinations.

Tom made a few trips with Burton with a load of props and helped load a few of the big noisy trucks. He hitched a ride on one of them down to Valley Head and went to the Post Office to see if he had any mail in his box. He had two letters from McBain, and in the second his chief has sent him his pay due to him in a Postal Money order. He debated the wisdom of cashing a $300.00 money order here so close to Mingo where it might cause comment as to why he was receiving that kind of money in the mail, and from Washington, D.C to boot. So upon consideration decided not to cash his pay just yet. McBain hoped he would be successful, he said in his letter, and bring the gang of moonshiners operating in that locality to justice. Also he was much concerned to hear of Bells misfortune about his being snake bitten, and was sure the people who had taken him in and nursed him back to health were good honest people, and could not possibly be the type of people who would be associated with the illegal manufacture of intoxicating beverages.

After reading his mail he wrote to his chief a brief report, but deliberately said he had nothing of interest to report at present. He had found work, he wrote, and was keeping his eyes and ears open. More than that he had nothing to say. He mentioned not a word about who he was staying with, or who he was working for. And of a certainty he was positive McBain would be interested to know his life had doubtless been saved by a drink of mountain whiskey. And then there was that night riding Burton and Debassius had done before cold weather had set in. Knowing the revenue chief as he did he felt reasonably sure McBain would comment that it was something shady, and worth investigating .

These things were his own private secrets, and he definitely didn't intend to let McBain, or any other agent like him, gain knowledge of them. They would look at the people of this mountain country as being nothing more or less than law breakers, if they were engaged in illegally manufacturing whiskey. In a sense they could be termed as such, then again in another sense they were but following age old customs that for generations had been handed down from father to son. But the cold blooded, political minded men who run the federal agencies would never for a moment look upon activities such as that as being an old family custom. Then again there was another angle to all this which he always frowned upon. As a revenue agent he had received invitations to parties, and get togethers thrown by the department and had attended some of them. He had been appalled at the things he had seen transpire at those gatherings. Half of the head men that had attended from the department had become exceedingly drunk before the party had broken up. The bottles of whisky had been produced from some mysterious source and had been lapped up like so much water. Considering their shameful conduct, who was the greater transgressor? The God-fearing, hard-working, hospitable, down-to-earth mountaineer,, in his quaint easy going way of life, or the cold blooded, shrewd, scheming, two-faced, political ruled, hypocrite who classed himself as an honest, law abiding citizen. The answer to that question was plain for all to see.

He would play the part yet a little longer,

Bell told himself. But of interest in his job, and all it pertained to, he had none. Long since that had ceased to be. In the spring, he would write McBain and resign. And wash his hands of the whole double-dealing mess. His paramount object now in life was to win completely the heart and hand of Jane Burton. He would carve himself a home here in this high country if she was by his side, as his wife. To lose this wonderful girl, now that he had found her, was unthinkable.

His day in Valley Head came to a close about three o'clock in the afternoon. He had made previous arrangements with the truck driver he had come down from Mingo with that morning to pick him up on his last trip to Mingo for the props that day. The driver had said that his last load would be loaded at a little after four o'clock and he would come through town around three p.m. So at nearly three o'clock he again boarded the heavy rumbling truck. The vehicle rode as rough as a road wagon, and made a terrible noise. All four tires being solid rubber did not improve its riding qualities. It went rumbling and roaring, and bouncing up the rutted road toward Mingo. Twenty miles an hour was the best speed it could maintain. Tom had bought a present for Jane and something useful for Mrs. Burton at the largest store the town could boast. Also he purchased some winter underwear and warm heavy clothing for the cold months ahead. For his employer, he bought a large tin of choice smoking tobacco. The Indian he remembered with a generous supply of ammunition for his gun and two bright colored plaid shirts. When he viewed all the things he had purchased for Jane's mother and father and Jim Debassius upon second thought he decided to buy another present for the big eyed girl he loved. Knowing her possessive nature, and loving her for it, if she had the slightest thought he was spending more on other presents than he did on her presents, how those wonderful eyes would flash, how that determined little chin would stand out, how hurt and reproachful the look she would bend upon him. So if being forewarned is being forearmed, he acted accordingly. He yearned to hold her in his arms in his every waking hour, therefore, nothing that might keep his heart's desire from realizing fulfillment.

Night time was settling over the high country when he arrived home. The day had been cold and cloudy but as daylight faded, the clouds parted in a number of places and stars began to peep out. By the time full darkness had come, countless numbers of the little and big lights of the heavens were ablaze. Being grateful for the protective darkness Tom hurried past the main residence of the Burton family, and entered the two room cabin he shared with the easy going taciturn Indian. The three hounds heralded his homecoming in a lusty voice, and when Jane came to the living room door to see what their commotion meant he was just closing the cabin door. After supper was over then he would hand out the presents and listen to the exclamations of delight. It would do his heart good to bring joy to these good people by his remembrance of them.

Supper was being put on the table when he entered the kitchen. Everybody was present and greeted him pleasantly. Burton spoke in his booming way, and inquired how Valley Head was. The Indian nodded and smiled. Jane and her mother momentarily halted their preparations of supper and remarked smilingly, "Glad to see you-all back home safe and sound."

"Thank you Jane and Mrs. Burton. I had a good trip, but never pick one of those big solid tire trucks for riding comfort. It's worse than riding in a road wagon."

"Haw, Haw," roared the mountaineer. "Shore' now an' them big heavy tracks should be most as comfortable as ridin' in a rockin' chair.

Looks like they'd hold the road good. What do you say Jim?"

"Well now," drawled that worthy. "Maybe Tom is sort of tender in spots. I admit I've rode things that were more – well – more agreeable to my feeling. An' then I've rode worse. But I more or less agree with Tom. They ain't built for comfort."

"See any purty gals son?" asked Burton with a big smile and broad wink.

"Yes, quite a few," answered Tom.

"Did they see you?" asked Jane in her laughing voice.

"Well I suppose so. One or two smiled at me when they passed me on the sidewalk. But of course, I wasn't interested. I had some buying of things to do."

"Pull up supper everybody," Burton said heartily. "I'm so hungry, I could eat the north end of a south bound hoss'. And I want to hear more about them purty gals." There upon Mrs. Burton smiled and glanced at her seemingly disinterested daughter. For all the outward sign the girl gave, one would gather that the subject of conversation was very boring to her. But it was noticeable her quick smile and gay laugh was abrupt, and seemed absorbed in her food.

"Well Mrs. Burton," Tom began. "I seen the

prettiest one of the pretty girls today in the biggest dry goods store in town. She was one of the clerks and waited on me. Her personality was delightful, and she was very charming."

"Make a date with her, Tom?" pursued the bearded man. "Shore' an' if I was a young buck again, an' foot loose an' fancy free, I'd have asked her if I could come a wooin'. A man is only a young rooster once you know."

Before Tom answered his employers last question about asking a date with the clerk, he glanced up from his plate towards Jane. Her eyes met his and seemed to convey a message of silent entreaty. It was impossible for him to kid about the attention other girls may have shown him, feeling about her the way he did. So when he answered the bearded giant he spoke directly from the heart.

"No I didn't. She was very nice and friendly and very good looking, but I wasn't interested. My heart belongs to some other pretty girl you see."

"What's this you say young feller?" spoke out Burton with evident interest. "Tell me about your lady love, an' I meant no offense by my kidding remarks. I'm always eager to hear about young love. I was smitten once by that fatal disease myself. Haw Haw."

"I can't tell you anything for sure right now, boss," answered Tom with a smile. "But one of these days I'll have a little talk with you about it.

Hope you will be able to see things as I see them when that time comes. Your good opinion will mean a lot to me."

"Why anytime at all, Bell. I'd be happy to talk over with you any problem you might have. And right now let me say you have my good wishes."

As Bell spoke to her father saying that his heart was already lost to someone else, Jane sat as one turned to stone. Presently she resumed her eating, but it seemed to cost her extreme effort to force her food down. A rosy tinge had stained her tanned cheeks, and when at last she glanced up and met his gaze again, Tom detected a shadowy far-away look in her big brown eyes. The conversation swung to other things. Eventually the evening repast was over and the mountain farmer reached into his shirt pocket for his vile smelling, big bowled, short stemmed pipe. Taking a small pocket knife from his pocket he opened the largest blade and proceeded to run its keen edge round inside the bowl of his huge pipe. A grating grinding sound was made. He turned the bowl upside down in the palm of his right hand and a small pile of half burned tobacco and charred fragments, and ashes fell into his palm. This rank, smelling stuff he threw into the kitchen stove. Then taking a twist of tobacco from a kitchen shelf Burton shaved a generous portion from it into his hand. When this was done he proceeded to close his pocket knife and cupping his hands together began to rub them together in a brisk rotating manner. This action pulverized the tobacco he had shaved from the twist.

When the big man had ceased to rub his hands together, he then took his pipe in his hands and proceeded to pour the fine tobacco in its large bowl, tramping it down with a forefinger the while. The pipe was then lit with a glowing ember from the hearth of the kitchen stove. Settling back he puffed clouds of white smoke upwards. A look of tranquil satisfaction seemed to steal over his relaxed form and bearded features. Debassius rolled himself a long thin cigarette. Jane and her mother began to clear the dishes from the table. Tom then decided it was the right time for him to go and bring forth his presents. So excusing himself he went across the yard to the two-roomed cabin and procured the package of presents he had bought in Valley Head that day. Returning to the kitchen he laid the sizable package on the floor by the door. Jane immediately inquired about its contents.

"My Tom," she remarked with shining eyes, "What a big package. You-all must of bought the store out, getting yourself so many winter things."

"Oh I bought a few things for myself to break the winter winds. But the things in this package lying on the floor is not for me."

"They're not? Then pray tell me who they're for."

"For you, and your parents, and Jim."

"Can I open it?" she asked. Her words

coming in a rush almost like a little child.

"Go ahead," he answered. "And I hope

everybody likes everything I purchased for them."

Burton looked at Tom and smiled. Taking

his pipe from his mouth he informed the revenue

man that if anybody was kind enough to buy him a

present, well he would be most happy to receive it.

Jane knelt by the package and unwrapped it.

The first tiding she took from it was the bright red

and green scarf and mittens set. Turning to Tom,

she held them up and inquired as to who they belonged to.

"Those are for you Jane. To keep your hands and neck warm this coming winter."

"Thank you-all for them Tom. They are the most beautiful ones I believe I've ever seen. Usually they always come in solid colors."

Delving back into the package the happy girl brought out a rather large bundle for him to see. She held it up.

"What is this Tom and who does it go to?" she asked.

"Oh, that is for your mother. Open the bundle up and see if she likes what I got for her."

"I'm sure I will," the good woman spoke out with a smile. Jane then unwrapped a half dozen towels. And a half dozen wash cloths to go with the towels and lastly two fine aprons were handed to her mother.

"Tom, Christmas is next month. Don't you know that? You're going to spoil this crowd giving them these things before then. But don't try to take them back now. I won't like to have to wait that long to try my new aprons. Thanks a lot."

"You're very welcome, Mrs. Burton," he told her. "Jane give your father what I bought him."

A pound box of tobacco was handed to the mountaineer. He boomed out his thanks, and immediately knocked out the tobacco he was then smoking in his pipe, then opening up his box of cut tobacco proceeded to fill his pipe from that. Another red ember was fished out of the stove hearth and placed upon the tobacco. He began to puff. The ember glowed like a ruby, and begun to eat its way into the tobacco. Soon his pipe was well lit. Taking the box of tobacco up in a large hand, he sniffed at it slowly. Raising his head he grinned at Tom and winked. "That's good stuff, young feller. If you was a smokin' man you'd enjoy a pipe of that. This box'll last me till way up in the winter, an' maybe most to spring. An' my thanks to you. Why don't you and Jim take tomorrow off from prop cuttin' an' take a turkey hunt? You both have my permission, but I refuse to go along. That long legged Jim near walked me to death a couple of falls back when I was foolish enough to go with him. But I said never again."

"It was a real pleasure to get the tobacco for you, boss. I enjoyed every minute of my shopping spree. And I'll be happy and very excited to go on a turkey hunt with Jim, that is if he wants to go and the weather permits. What you say Jim?" Tom asked the silent Indian.

"O. K by me except for one thing," he answered in his lazy southern drawl.

"An' what might that one thing be Jim?"

inquired the bearded Burton.

"We don't have enough shells for our guns to go huntin'," came the reply. As the Indian statement about being short on ammunition Tom was conscious of an inward thrill. He decided to play it up big before playing his trump card. Because that very day he had purchased the silent Jim a generous supply of ammunition for all the guns he possessed. So acting down in the mouth and very much put out he turned to his cabin partner and said in his best tone of disappointment, "I'd have loved to have gone out on a turkey hunt with you Jim but if you have no shells that's that, and I can't go. Would you have liked to have gone if we weren't out of ammunition?"

"Oh shore', I would be up an' rarin' to go about daylight. That's my ticket. Get out after them big birds just as they are getting off the roost. All full of sleep, an' a big desire to scratch up the leaves an' fill their craws with nuts, and bugs, and worms, an' whatever else hungry turkeys like for breakfast. Too bad we ain't got enough shells. Guess we'll have to out props an' spank our mules."

"I'll go get a couple of boxes down to Mingo tomorrow boys," interposed the mountaineer. "If you-all are goin' on a turkey hunt this fall it's high time to go. We could have half a yard of snow up on them ridges any night from now on. An' down here in the lower ground too."

"Yes, that's true," Tom said with a long face and a quick wink at Jane.

"If that comes it'll mean no turkey hunting for us this fall."

"Jim, are you-all sure you ain't playin' off lazy and not out of shells at all?" Jane suddenly asked the lounging Debassius. At her words he looked surprised and then hurt. And a look of injured pride crossed his usually placid features. Spreading wide his hands he raised his eyebrows and shrugged his shoulders. "Honest to God Janie girl, in fact I'd insist on goin' if we had the shells an' that's a fact."

"On your word of honor Jim Debassius,

you-all ain't tryin' to just play off that away?"
pursued the smiling girl. She had evidently
interpreted the meaning of Tom's wink as meaning
he had something up his sleeve. And she was
absolutely right. Again the young Indian stated the
reason behind their not being able to go. Then
added –

"Just show me a box of thirty-thirty shells
for my rifle, and a box of 16 gauge shotgun shells
for my double barrel, and you'd have to tie me up
to keep me home tomorrow. Even tho' my feet are
fair killin' me I'd not hesitate a minute from
goin'." When the Indian made his last statement,
Tom and Jane laughed aloud and looked at each
other and winked.

"Well Janie, since Jim feels that way about the hunt I say give him the presents I bought for him in Valley Head today."

Mr. and Mrs. Burton had not been listening to the cross questioning of the Indian by Jane and Tom. And of their evident desire for him to commit himself in a way where he couldn't back out if he had any shells for the guns. A broad smile crossed their faces as Jane lifted out a square package, from the bigger package on the floor, and deposited it on the table with a solid thudding sound. She slid it across the table to where Jim was, half sitting, and half lying, in his chair. Almost it seemed he was really sitting at times on his neck. With an inquiring look upon his lean hawk-like face a strong slim brown hand slid up over the edge of the table and grasped the mysterious package. Hand number two followed the first, and between his concentrated efforts the package was soon opened. One glance at the contents of it and a knowing grin crossed the Indians dark face.

"Shore' now Tom," he drawled. "I'm bettin' my hard earned cash right here an' now that you an' Jane cooked up this trap for me between you-all."

"You're laying your money wisely Jim," laughed Tom. "I was the one who trapped. Jane didn't know I was loaded for you till I winked at her a moment ago. After that the rest was easy."

"Jim do you-all feel well?" inquired Jane. "The way you've been tryin' to dodge goin' huntin' tomorrow I've more or less come to the conclusion you're sick, or something. How about it?"

"I ain't exactly sick, but my legs an' feet have been hurtin' me all day. Maybe I never told any of you this, but I had a kind of rheumatism when I was a boy. The kind that hits the little kids. I got over it in time, nearly so that is, but my feet and legs bother me a lot at some times. Specially' in cold wet weather. An' at times of the year like in the fall and spring, when it's cold and wet an' not too hot of days."

"Well now Jim, I've very sorry to hear of your ailment. And you have my sympathy," Tom spoke up. "And we'll forget about the turkey hunt we had talked about. Go some other time when you're feeling up to par. O.K.?"

"We'll go if I feel able to travel at all by mornin'," declared the Indian. "Maybe by then I'll feel like my old self again. Who can tell?"

"Gosh I hope so," Tom returned. "I've always read and dreamed about hunting wild turkeys in the mountains, and up till now it has remained a dream. I was hoping I'd be able to make my dreams come true this fall."

"Well Jim if you an' Tom can't go tomorrow, I'm for lettin' you two go when you feel up to it," Burton boomed out. "You-all can cut an' saw, an' split, an' pile props all winter, weather permittin', but now is the time to take a crack at them old fat gobblers back there in the woods. Them old birds have crammed their craws all fall with plenty of food, an' I'm willing to say right out there goin' to be fat as a roll of butter. How's your idea of that Jim?"

"You're speakin' wisdom Lige," answered Debassius in a low voice. "But try an' sneak up on the old boys an' gals. They can hear you-all an' see you-all an' I say they can even spot a man by smellin' him. Yes, they're fat an' sassy now, an' I'll do my best to bring us home a couple of nice ones. If I'm able that is."

"Tom this big package on the floor isn't

empty yet. What else is in it?" Jane inquired eagerly.

"Look and see," he replied.

The rosy cheeked girl delved again into the bundle on the floor. This time she brought forth a large squarish package. She looked at Tom inquiringly and he pointed to Debassius. Handing over the bundle to him she again explored the bottom of the paper package by her chair. Another wrapped gift was found therein. Tom looked at her and grinned, then pointed his forefinger of his right hand at her. A happy light sprang into her wonderful eyes, and the man who gave her the gift ached to hold her to his breast an cover her dear face with hungry kisses.

With eager trembling hands the girl undid the wrappings on the last package. A gasp of pleasant surprise came from her parted lips when its contents lay exposed. A box of chocolates, two pound size, lay on top. Laying that aside she picked up a silk head scarf, a box of handkerchiefs, a bottle of perfume, and a card. Opening the card she found it to be a friendship card.

"Tom Bell, you-all are one wasteful person," she told him with a frown creasing her forehead. "Spending your money recklessly this way." A happy smile took possession of her features. "I thank you-all very much for your wonderful gifts. But I agree with mother. Christmas ain't till next month an' then you-all will be havin' to buy presents all over again. It was good of you to think of all of us this way though."

"Every one of you are very welcome I'm sure. It was a pleasure for me to spend money to make other people happy besides myself for a change," Tom spoke earnestly. "The least I can do is to try and show my appreciation for all you people have done for me in some small way. I wouldn't be here tonight if you hadn't extended your hands to me in my hour of need."

"Aw – hell – now son," boomed out the big mountaineer. "We only did for you what we'd expect people to do for any one of us were we ever to be in a like situation."

"Us mountain people might seem a little queer to outsiders at first," Mrs. Burton said. "But we do believe in an' practice the Golden Rule in our lives, much as we can."

"Personally I think you're wonderful," answered the revenue man. "And I always will, no matter how you try to make light of your services to me."

Everybody laughed at this last statement of Toms, and then centered their attention on the cool, easy, lazy appearing, Debassius. They all three called to him to open his present. It lay unopened in his lap. A faraway, meditating, look had crept into his piercing black eyes. "Tom I'm thankin' you-all for the shells an' whatever else you got for me," he drawled. "If I'm up to par tomorrow we'll go on a wild goose chase. Only we'll be huntin' wild turkeys an' I'm hopin' for good weather an' good huntin'. Now I'll open up my package that's killin' this big eyed Jane to see inside of." And with his low expressive chuckle, the Indian unwrapped the package laying in his lap and held up the two plaid shirts. Watching his prop cutting buddies closely Tom devised he was pleased with everything, because a slow grin changed the hawk like quality of his still immobile face. At sight of the bright colored shirts, Jane gave a cry of surprise and walked over to examine them closely.

"My but they're pretty, an' so warm lookin'," she cried out running her small well-formed hands over the fuzzy, bright colored, crossbar red shirts. "Jim, this comin' winter if it gets real cold, could I borrow these warm shirts till the weather moderates?"

"Well now reckon you-all could," he replied. "That is providing you'll lend me your scarf an' gloves. I want to keep from freezin' to death in zero weather myself you know. Haw, Haw."

"An' what would I be doin' for something to keep my hands an' neck warm with about that time, Jim Debassius?" she asked him with her wonderful flashing eyed look. He gave her a cool easy grin in return. An inevitable chuckle fell on her listening ears.

"I was thinkin' Jane about what you could

do in a case like that, an' I've come up with what I consider to be a peach of a solution. Want to hear it?" he asked lazily.

"Naturally, Jim. Spill it," came her instant response to his inquiry.

"Here's my solution," he slowly replied. "When you're wearin my nice warm shirts, an' I'm wearin your nice new warm mittens an' scarf, you-all can make out just fine. Put your hands in your pockets and wrap an old burlap sack round your neck. How does that strike you-all?"

"Great idea. Just great. But Jim I think you-all would be better suited to something like a sack for a scarf than I would. 'Cause your neck is much

longer than mine, an' you could get a fine wrappin'
job done on it with a big old rough sack. What do
you think about it? Don't you see my point there?"
And with their exchange of kidding her silvery
laugh rang out. Tom an' Mr. and Mrs. Burton
joined in the laugh. The Indian laughed also and
spoke in his drawling way.

"Dog-gone it Jane, you always beat me in
something like this cause my neck is longer than
most. I'll have to think it over whether I'd better
risk my health in real cold weather, lendin' out my
warmest shirts like that. Why I might wind up
havin' pneumonia. I still say you'd look good
wrapped up in a sack though. Haw, Haw."

The Indian rose from his chair to his full

lean length. And going into the living room, which adjoined the kitchen, came back out with his short heavy jacket on and a batter felt hat on his head.

"It's time I hit the hay folks," he informed them. "Maybe I'll feel more up to par by morning. Jane you-all can't go on this turkey hunt. My great fear is that you'd bag one of the old boys before I did an' if that ever happened, I'd never be able to live it down."

"Why Jim, you-all know I shoot a gun something terrible. Honestly I couldn't hit the side of a barn. You've nothing to fear."

"Oh no? I know that. Nothing at all," he scoffed at her. "Remember last time we was target practicing, I thought I did well but when little Jane took the twenty-two and bore down on the target it was drilled dead center, an' most every time."

"Aw Jim, that was only a lucky day," she remonstrated with him. "I'd probably not get to throw any lead at a turkey if I could persuade you and Tom to take me along. An' I'd be quiet as a little ole mouse, and not argue with you-all about a thing." Turning to Tom she cast the full force of her magnetic eyes directly into his own in a long look of silent pleading. Who could resist this girl's will power, he asked himself. His love for her made him only the more susceptible to her pleading. So he decided to leave the decision of her going with them up to Debassius. In other words he knew he was passing the buck, but he honestly hoped Jim would consent to taking her along. In her presence he was happy, no matter what.

"Tom," she began in her best wheedling voice. "Say I can go. I know you-all want me along. Why Jim here never would take me on a turkey hunt, an' he has always come home with a nice fat one, sometimes two."

"Jane I can't go against Jim's wishes," Bell told her regretfully. "He will be boss from the time we enter the woods back up the valley on that high ridge. Personally I'd be very happy to have you with us, but it's up to him."

The Indian shifted from side to side.

Obviously the decision was a hard one for him. He looked toward the girls' parents and Tom was thrilled to see one eyelid drop in a significant wink. He winked again at the mountaineer and wife, an' turning his head squarely toward the expectant girl again resumed his attitude of unconcerned refusal. A hot argument on the part of Jane ensued. Reasons why she should go were given in her best persuasive manner. In like turn the Indian voiced numerous reasons why she shouldn't go. Tom and Mr. and Mrs. Burton listened and laughed. After a while it became noticeable that Debassius' arguments were getting weaker and quick to sense the trend Jane waxed more eloquent. At last the Indian shrugged his shoulders and threw his hands into the air in evident surrender.

"Well now Janie girl," he drawled at her. "You have my consent to go on the turkey hunt tomorrow. That is if we go. But you needn't have put up such a scandalous bunch of reason on why you should go. 'Cause I was willing from the first that you could go, along if you wanted to I mean. Good night, see you-all in the morning." And with a deep chuckle he opened the kitchen door and stepped into the darkness outside.

A flush of spirit dyed the oval face of Jane Burton. Then the humor of it all struck her and her contagious laughter pealed out.

"That miserable devilish wretch," she said to her parents and Tom. "I'll do my best to get the first shot at a turkey tomorrow if I possibly can. That'll even up the score."

"Well, guess I'll hit the hay myself folks," rolled out Burton in his hearty voice. "I'm not going on any wild goose chase myself tomorrow, but I can still use all the sleep I can lay my hands on."

"I'm tired myself," Mrs. Burton spoke out. "That washin' me an' Jane done up today sort of fagged me out. So paw' reckon' I'll be hitting' the hay too."

"Tom, are you-all as tired out as Jim an' Mother an' Dad?" asked Jane.

"No I'm not what you could call exhausted. I could probably go to sleep if I was in bed maybe, why do you ask?"

"I thought maybe we could play some checkers an' pop some corn or go for a walk. It is only nine o'clock, an' ten thirty is plenty early to go to bed. That would give a person seven hours sleep till five thirty in the morning. Would you-all like to do some of the things I've mentioned?"

"I'd be delighted Jane," he answered quickly. "That is providing we have the permission of your father and mother."

"Oh, go ahead you two," Burton said. "Don't think I'll care about the good sleep you two lose, cause' I'll be gettin' enough of it myself."

"Thank you, Mr. Burton," the revenue man replied. "Jane knows we both have a hunting trip planned, and we can play checkers an' popcorn some other evening. But I want to see what kind of a checker player Jane is, how about that Jane? Are you champion of this home?"

"Naturally," the mountain girl answered. "An' I'm lookin' for another victim to add to my list. Ain't you-all a little bit afraid to play checkers with me? You do play them don't you Tom?"

"I've played a couple of games in my life," he replied. "Get the board and checkers and start the battle. But I'm warning you right now I'll be out for your hide from the first, as we used to say about this game."

"If you-all think I'll be givin' the games away maybe you've a little surprise comin'," she told him flashily. Her father and mother burst out laughing as she went into the living room for the board and checkers. In a moment she returned with it, and the round discs called checkers. Pulling up their chairs close together they lay the board on the kitchen table between them.

Thinking that he might test her knowledge of the game, Tom turned the board round and round pretending to be examining it. Actually his purpose was to leave his double corners on his left, while he knew full well that the double corner of a checker board is always to a players' right.

Jane stopped sorting out the red and black discs of wood. Pushing his pile over to him he saw that she had chosen the red one. Obviously she believed she played a better game with a bright color, because at that moment she spoke up saying that her choice of checkers was always the red ones. Adding that red seemed to be her lucky color.

Then her attention became fastened upon the board. Without a moment's hesitation, she grasped it in a firm tanned hand and swung it round till her double corners was at her right hand. Then she placed her red checkers in position. He did likewise. Looking at each other, they both smiled and each wished the other good luck.

"Reckon I'll take the first move, Mr. Bell," Jane spoke sweetly. "A courtesy always shown women players you know." And reaching squarely into the center of her positioned men she shoved one forward. The game began quietly, slowly, unhurried, with scarcely any excitement.

In a few moments of playing Tom realized he was up against a skillful player. Somehow she seemed to group her men in such a fashion that they began marching across the board in a solid front. Not a break appeared in her defense line.

Tom spearheaded his men in order that he might break through her line. He had just gotten his men in position when she unconcernedly showed a red colored man up to one of his black ones. He jumped the red one only to be jumped immediately in return. The girl began to hammer at his line of men. After a few exchanges of men, she pulled a slick move on him. Up ahead he had two men in position to be jumped if only she had a man of his in position close enough to force him to jump her. It was her move again, and the big eyed girl seemed to consider long upon it. Then with a toss of her chestnut brown hair, Jane gave him a man of hers in exchange for one of his. This action put a man of his in a position where she could give him another checker and take three of his. That way she was trading two for three. In short it was slick checker playing. A look of appreciation crept into Tom's eyes at her skill. Always his keenest pleasure in this gaze was to best a worthy opponent. And this girl he loved promised to be such a one.

By her latest move Jane had a man in position to become a king. If this king was allowed to live it would prove disastrous to him. So at the first opportunity he fed a private into the face of Mr. King and copped off him the board. Jane muttered under her breath at his play. The fight waged back and forth, and in time they both had five kings. Then a skillful battle ensued. By skillful maneuvering the girl finally induced him to move into a trap. The instant he fell for his bait, he saw his mistake. She knew he was in the soup, and looking up gave him a wide grin. A trade was made. Only she came out of the trade with two of his men to only one of hers lost. Now she had four to his three.

"Mr. Bell, if my memory is not on the blink you-all told me you was out for my hide in this game," she told him with a wide grin on her pretty face. "Well, I'm right now goin' to do a little hide collectin' myself."

At her words Tom knew his chances were doomed. Her father and mother looked at them and laughed. Then rose form their chairs and saying good night left the kitchen. Two even trades of men swiftly followed. He now had but one man left, and she armed with two. A chase to his double corner followed. Skillfully she made her moves and in a very little while he was forced to move up out of this retreat. He started once more across the board, toward her double corner. But she paced him evenly and when he came to where he had to move out of where he had wound up, she was sitting there waiting for him like a cat waiting for a mouse. He had lost the first game. Two more followed quickly and he lost one of those.

She had a score now of two best out of three, and was evidently greatly pleased. If he was to beat this girl at playing checkers Tom became convinced he had to study his every move carefully, and be crafty as a fox. He made a mental promise to do this in the long winter months ahead.

"Tom do you want to play anymore checkers this evening?" Jane asked him, at the conclusion of the third game. "Or do you think you'd like some nice hot popcorn?"

"I'll take the popcorn now Janie girl and skin you alive at this game later on," he answered at once. Soon she had a pan full of the snowy, fluffy delicious corn before him. They ate in silence and he noticed she seemed restless. Soon as the popcorn was gone, she immediately fetched his coat and hat and her coat and new mitten and scarf set. "Let's go for a little walk Tom," she said softly in a way that made his blood leap. They had scarcely gotten clear of the yard when the girl stopped and pulling his head down kissed him fiercely.

"There now," she said. "How's that for payment for bestin' you-all at checkers this evenin'?"

"That is wonderful payment, you darling," he answered her immediately. "I'll confess though, you sure fooled me at that game. I used to be pretty good at it myself once, but honey to be honest with you, you've got me skinned a-block."

"Oh Tom Bell don't talk like that," she said exasperated. "You-all could beat me good and plenty I know. All you need is a little bit of practice. I don't mind a bit when you beat me. Honest I don't. But I never felt that way when anybody laid the wood to me."

"Honey let's walk a bit down the road," he suggested softly to her.

"O.K we'll walk down the road a-ways, but I just know I can read your mind," came her reply. "My wager says you-all want to kiss me an' hug me a lot. Tom, I could feel them things in the way you-all looked at me this evenin', an' the sound of your voice. It sounded sort of – well – sort of husky an' low an' a lot like a caress or something." All he did in reply was to swing his arm around her and start walking with her slowly down the rutted road. Silently Jane tripped lightly along in the circle of his arms. When they were a goodly distance from her home, he stopped by a pile of props Burton had piled off a load by the roadside.

"It's cold outside tonight, honey, but let's set here awhile," came his request, "do you mind?"

"Of course not," she told him softly. "I don't mind a little cold now an' then. If I do get cold, why you-all could play the gallant gentleman an' take me in your arms an' sort of protect me from the chill winds. What say?"

"Its wonderful little girl. Just like you. Now come here an' set beside me and let me fold you tightly into my arms. You read my mind correctly Janie girl and I say this much. I've kept myself straight as I possibly could in this life and been as honest as possible. But sometimes I get to longing so much to hold you tight against my breast that I would not stop to remember to be gentle with the little person I love. Right now my darling, I'd like so very much to hold you so tight you could hardly breathe. I'm in love with you, or have you forgotten that?"

"I'll never forget your honest way of telling me of your love," Jane said to Tom as she crept close to him on the prop pile where he was sitting. "But as I've said I'm not just sure in my mind yet about marriage. Be patient, an' I'll probably know for sure by warm weather next spring."

"What time is the spring do you call warm weather, Jane darling?" Tom inquired. "How late is that?"

"Well, by the middle of June at the latest."

"And suppose you've decided by then not to

have my as your future husband. What'll I do then?"

"Let's not cross any bridges till we get to them Tom," she said, laying her sweet cool right hand across his lips. While it reposed there he kissed it several times. Smilingly he patted his lips.

"Janie girl, there's something I want to ask you," the revenue man said to her presently.

How swiftly she looked into his face. How searching her clear wide-eyes gaze. Looking down into her upturned anxious little face, almost it seemed to Bell as if she expected him to take her into his confidence. With cold hands she clasped his wrists, and in a whispering voice inquired of him what it was he wanted to talk to her about.

"It's about him," he began. "I've noticed his eyes upon you a lot lately. In their depths seemed to be a smoldering fire. My guess is that he's in love with you. He's always treated me fine, but being around him a lot like I am, I notice these things. What do you think about it?"

"Does it make you jealous Mr. Bell to think another man might be in love with me? After all, I'm not exactly an old beat up bag of bones yet a while. But to be honest I've always known Jim is more or less interested in me. And him bein' an Indian might make him seem more than usual possessive of a female. He's a straight-forward fellow. So please don't be surprised if he wants to set down one of these days an' have a talk with you about all this. If he does, it'll be only his way of going at things."

"I'll be happy to talk with him any time he's in the mood. He knew you, and no doubt loved you, for years now. And I can understand how he must feel. My heart goes out to him. But I'm not going to step aside for any man long as you're still footloose and fancy free. I want you for my very own Janie dear, do you blame me for feeling that way?"

"I can't blame you in the least. Sure know I'd never step aside just because another girl might be interested in you. I'm very fond of Jim, but I'm by no means in love with him. He has often spoke of an Indian girl down in the Big Smokies, where you were raised, that has had her eye on him for quite some time. Maybe he'll go back to his girl someday. My hunch is that they were sweethearts once. He's never said so but I've always gathered as much."

"Jim has always struck me as being an' honest dependable fellow," Tom said. "And I think he'll make a good husband for a girl. Now don't think me narrow minded, Janie honey, for my viewpoint on this matter, but my personal opinion is that if he has an old sweetheart in the Big Smokies whose still pining for him, he'll be a happier man to marry her then if he married a girl who is not of his nationality or creed."

"What's the way I've always looked at it. Ever since I've been old enough to know about things like that. He tells me his old sweetheart's name is Daisy Dell Hansbraugh. An' she is in her early twenties by now. He always said she was beautiful too. By the way Tom Bell, do you-all still see me as being beautiful?"

"It's hard to describe my feelings for you little girl. Now about me. I personally consider you as being much too pretty a girl to become attached to an old rundown fellow like me. You are beautiful, and in a lot of ways that I can't describe. Now let's talk about you and me some. Do you want me to kiss you and hug you tonight? You didn't exactly say, so I'd like for you to set me straight."

She gave him an impish look, which in the pale glow from the stars and half-moon partially lit up her face. He encircled her once more with his arms and held her close, waiting for an answer to his question. A reply was coming forthwith.

"If you-all can tell me how I want to have you kiss an' hug me – well I say I pity you. Don't get the wrong impression of me. I'm sure not trying to string you-all along, I'll give you an honest answer to any question you want to ask me about, one of these beautiful mountain days. So till then Tom I can't say more. But I've been thinking serious about us, an' I think I'll go have a little talk with Preacher Kane. He always said I was his daughter, an' any an' all who should think otherwise'll have to answer to him"

"I want to have some long talks with that kindly old philosopher of life myself," Tom told her, "and if he tells me things I don't want to hear I'll feel like crowning him. Mrs. Kane is a kindly, silent, pleasant old lady. Her hair is white as snow, and she reminds me of my own mother some. By her general appearance, her kindly way, and thoughtfulness and that certain indescribable something all good mothers have."

"I've a good mother an' father. They're always been kind, an' loving, an' good to me. Guess I'm luckier than lots of girls. I've often wondered what it would be like to have brothers an' sisters. But I never set around an' worry much about it."

"You're a darling girl Jane. And your parents are fortunate to have a fine daughter like you. We'd better be going back to the house. It's too cold to set here. You and I might get sick. First though I want to kiss the girl I love a couple of times or so. You have only yourself to blame if I pester you with kisses every chance I get. You shouldn't have made me fall in love with you. I was sick and couldn't help myself so I hold you personally responsible." At his words she turned so she was directly facing him, and smiled up into his eyes. "I'm glad if I made you-all fall in love with me," the smiling mountain girl murmured. "That's one thing I'll never be sorry for. Was I a bossy old thing when you-all was sick? I tried not to be, but I just felt inside I had some right to boss you around, I was your nurse, an' did for you best as I could. Did I treat you-all badly?"

He refrained from answering her with words. Instead he rose from his seat on the pile of props, and bending over the girl pulled her to her feet and into his hungry arms. With a leap of his heart, he was acutely aware of her arms creeping up around his neck. Surely she loves me as I love her, he told himself in that moment. Her head fell back. Her face gleamed pale and devastatingly beautiful in the shadowy starlight and the dim light cast by the moon. Small clouds had begun to run across the sky. As one of these would slide between the moon and the earth, her face was very shadowy. Then when the cloud was past the moon it came into sharper relief, with parted soft lips, only inches below his own.

"Forgive me darling if I seem rough to you, but I'm a man in love, and you're the object of my affections." And with these words Tom began kissing that lovely upturned face. Her arms tightened around his neck. She rose on tiptoe, and was soon meeting his lips, kiss for kiss. His ardor was such that he was considerable rough in this hugging and kissing of the girl in his arms. But of his roughness she complained not a word. In truth the more ardent he became the more pliant and subtle her response. Her instant kissing back, her clinging, tightening arms, her pressing pliant body, all these were undeniable proof to the revenue man that Jane Burton loved him.

Finally her face was brought hard against his thumping, throbbing heart. Her arms slid from round his neck to clasp him round the chest. A few moments they stood there while he kissed the top of her head. Then she stepped back and again looked up into his eyes. He bent to kiss her lips again. She began to speak in a low trembling voice. Her words seemed to be spoken with extreme difficulty. "Tom I can't let you-all kiss me that way again. I seem to lose myself in your arms. An' in truth I don't want to keep from losing myself in the spell of our kiss. Oh, Tom, Tom, one thing I must say to you-all. Please be honest with me in all things. I'm just what you see me here. A bewildered mountain girl trying desperately to hold onto part of her heart. We must know each other for what we are before we can hope to build any foundation for future happiness. My pride won't let me give my heart to any man who won't be completely honest with me. And so Tom honey ain't there anything you'd like to talk about with me? Maybe I seem prying to you-all but I can't help myself. I got to know."

For a long moment Tom Bell felt as one turned to stone. Her crying voice had hit him as an unfortunate blow. It could not be thrust aside in his mind any longer, this girl before him knew he was a federal agent. Quickly he formulated a plan in his mind. He'd spend the winter, still with his lips sealed, and in the spring he'd go and have a man to man talk with Old Preacher Kane. Instinctively he felt that the kindly old man who preached Gods' word to these mountain people would understand his predicament, and would maybe be able to help him. If Kane would be on his side, when he bared his heart to him, then he would confess all to Jane Burton and throw himself upon her love and pray that she would still love him and understand.

"Jane, Jane, please don't look at me so," he entreated her. "I'm not an escaped convict or a hoodlum. You are right dear girl, there's something I must tell you about myself before I'd ever let you marry me. I'll be perfectly honest with you, even at the risk of my own life. I see the people and things in this mountain country differently now. So darling girl, if in the end you turn away from me it'll be knowing in your heart of hearts that I love you and have come clean with you – in everything.

I ask you now, my love, to only believe in me. To trust me, because I'd lay down my life before I'd ever for a moment see you hurt, because of me, in any way. Tell me sweetheart, can I be more fair with you?" While he had been earnestly talking to her Jane had stood perfectly still, with her big brown eyes searching his shadowy face. At his question she stepped into his outstretched arms and clasped him to her. He kissed her tenderly.

"I'll wait till you-all want to tell me everything you-all think the girl you want to marry should know. If there's something on your mind that bothers you; why not go and have a talk with Preacher Kane. He told me he liked you, an' my daddy swears by the old Preacher for being truthful, an understandin' of peoples' problems, an' ways to find out solutions for them."

"You're right honey. I'll go and talk with Kane before long and I'll tell you about what we talk about and what he says. So till then please don't invite me to go with you on any more walks. 'Cause I'm only human and I love you so much. So in the face of all that I can't keep my arms from around you honey every time we take a walk alone after dark. Come on now, let's go back to the house."

Giving him a reassuring squeeze the girl turned away from the pile of props and taking him by the arm began walking toward home. Words were not needed to convey how these two young people felt about each other as they slowly strolled along. Unlinking her arm from his Tom put his arm around her shoulders and drew her close to him as they trudged along the uneven surfaced road. The night had turned considerable colder and the water in the ruts of the road were wearing a surface of ice. The mud had frozen in a crunchy crust and didn't stick to their shoes.

Soon the Burton residence was reached. As they came abreast of the kitchen door, Jane quickly turned and raised her face for a last kiss. Then softly saying goodnight she slipped inside, and closed the kitchen door. Tom thoughtfully strode across the yard to the cabin he shared with the Indian. A dim light was burning in the front room where the big open fireplace was. As he entered he seen it came from the lantern. Jim had it setting on the stool between their beds, and the flame turned down low.

Since the weather had turned colder, both beds had been moved into the same room. On cold winter nights to come, they could make use of the black yawning fireplace. The Indian lay prone and silent upon his bed. His long form wrapped in heavy blankets and homemade quilts. If he was aware of Tom's entry he gave no sign. His even breathing continued, unbroken, quietly, thoughtfully, and with troubled, furrowed brow the revenue man undressed and softly crept into his bed.

The next morning Tom was awakened by the booming voice of Lige Burton. He was bending over the bed and shaking the revenue man by the shoulder. "Roll out son," he boomed. "The days broke, an' Jim's rarin' to go. Jane is ready too. Between the two of them they say you're the biggest sleepy heads in these parts. Breakfast is ready an' waitin', so hurry an'throw your duds on." "I'll be ready in a jiffy," Tom yawned and shook his head to clear it of sleep. The big man laughed and turning round walked with his heavy tread from the cabin. Tom threw back the blankets and hurriedly dressed. Gray daylight was showing through the windows. He walked to the windows and looked out through the pane toward the east. A pink glow on the top of the distant timbered ridge heralded the rising sun. The day promised to be clear and doubtless cold. A heavy coating of frost lay over everything within his vision. Turning from the window he walked to the door and let himself outside. He could smell the odor of coffee and bacon on the still cold air, and lost no time crossing to the kitchen and entering. Breakfast was cooking on the kitchen stove, which was fairly dancing with the roaring fire burning on it.

"Good morning sleepy head," Jane sang out with a laugh. "Maybe you-all was out huntin' turkeys in your dreams. Tell us did you have any luck?"

"Good morning everybody," Tom said. "Sorry I'm late but I just couldn't seem to wake up. How do you feel this morning Jim? Do you feel as good as you look? I was loading up on sleep for todays' hike Janie."

"Well now," verily drawled Debassius. "Reckon as how I've decided to go on that goose chase today. An' Jane looks as if she could out run the longest legged old gobbler to be found in the woods."

"Good morning Jane," Tom said, and looked squarely into her big brown eyes and smiled. She gave him a gladsome smile in return. To him, as always the girl before him with her flowered apron round her waist looked wonderful. Mrs. Burton spoke pleasantly, and told him to get washed for breakfast. Which he promptly did. Soon they all were eating the hot steaming food. Hot white corn meal cakes, molasses, corn butter, bacon, fried boiled potatoes, and black coffee, sugar and cream made up the menu of the morning meal. He was surprised at the appetite he had developed since his entry into this mountain country. Back in the bustling metropolis of the nation's capital it would have been impossible for him to have consumed so much food for breakfast. But here in this pure clear high country air he seemed to be always hungry. And everything he ate agreed with him. While he resided in the city he knew what he could eat, and what he couldn't eat, with no unpleasant effects. Now all that picked diet routing was a thing of the past. And as he ate he was conscious of a humble gratefulness of feeling toward this mountaineer and his family.

"By the way who beat who at checkers last night?" Mrs. Burton inquired of Jane and Tom. Her husband and the Indian looked at the two in question with wide grins on their faces.

"You tell your mother Jane," Tom requested.

"I'd rather you-all told her and them two whose faces are all smiles," she replied. "But since you-all want me to I'll just say we both beat. He beat me and I beat him. Now how's that?"

"Fine," Debassius said. "But what we're cravin' to know is how many games was played an' who got the biggest number of them. I don't hear you-all braggin' much Jane, my guess is that for once you got skinned. Haw, Haw."

"I just as well come clean first as last," Tom

spoke out. "Jane laid me among the sweet peas twice out of three games. I might do better with a little practice, but my personal opinion is that she could take of herself no matter how much I practiced."

Debassius gave a mocking grin and bowed lightly to her from where he sat. "Reckon as it stands you-all are still the big cheese at checkers round here. But maybe you-all lose your crown someday."

Jane laughed merrily at the Indian's mocking grin and stiff little bow. When she spoke laughter still was in her voice.

"My most humble apologies to you Jim an'

everyone else for winnin' more games of checkers then I have lost. But somehow I feel I'll go on doin' exactly the same thing."

"If I weren't such a big blockhead myself I'd trim you-all girlie at that provokin' game," interposed her father. "Right now though I've work to do an'll have to be shovin' along. Hope you three bring home the bacon today in the form of a nice big fat gobbler. I'll do my share of eatin' of him to keep him from goin' to waste."

And without further preamble the bearded man retired from the breakfast table and putting on his coat and hat stepped to the door and let himself outside.

"Tell daddy not to work too hard at prop haulin' today," Jane said to her mother. "I'd help him but I've looked forward so long to goin' on a turkey hunt that now that I can go I better go. Jim might change his mind the next time you know." Mrs. Burton smilingly nodded her head.

"Well pardners', my motto has always been that the early bird gets the worm," the Indian stated. "So I'm fer' movin' our stumps a little on the rapid side. They live way back in the hills, an' don't take much interest in human affairs. It's daylight outside now an' I want to get into the woods before sun up. Right this minute them big birds are off their roosts an' huntin' across any grub worms, bugs, ants, an' the like that are buried deep enough to escape the frost. So let's don our gear an' be on our way."

Unanimous account was given to the suggestion made by Debassius. Quickly they made themselves ready for the trail. A lunch was packed in a small compact bundle. Guns were checked over and oiled. They could load their firearms when the woods were reached. All three carried shot guns, and had shells loaded with heavy shot. The previous day Tom had bought ammunition for all the guns while at Valley Head. In a matter of minutes, they were headed up the little valley. Their objective was the section where they had brought the big bear to bay half a month earlier.

The November sun was topping the timbered ridges when they reached the crest of the ridge above the cove where the ewes had fallen victim to the old bear. It came up from out of the eastern sky like a big round bell of fire. Long golden slanting rays shot forth from this greatest of lights. The tops of the second growth timber immediately began to catch the golden sunlight. While down at the bases of the trees the white frost clung to the leaves and up along the trunks.

At the crest of the ridge before beginning the ascent to the stream way down in the woods, the Indian held up a lean brown hand to command a halt. Turning round he admonished Tom and Jane to be as quiet as they possibly could from then on during the hunt. He informed them that they were hunting the varies of game birds and a very quiet approach was of the utmost importance.

At Jim's instructions, Jane shrugged her shoulders and gave him a raised eyebrow look. Then at his serious face, a wide grin spread across her oval countenance. At this by-play between the two, Tom could not but smile.

Without another word Debassius strode forth in to the trees. He moved forward very fast to be so quiet. His booted feet seemed always to step on rocks or solid ground. Not a twig did he snap as he glided along. Tom and Jane followed after him, keeping as quiet as they possibly could. The Indian swung to the right so as to miss the edge of the stand of virgin timber, and bore steadily downhill.

Occasionally he would stop and examine

signs turkeys had made recently. Obviously he was looking for fresh scratchings and diggings made by the big birds in the leaves and leaf mold. The revenue man paid close attention to one of the wild turkey signs they came across, and was much surprised to see how far down the ground was tore up. His guess would have been that these birds were tearing up the loose top soil, leaves, and leaf mold, to a depth of three or four inches. How strong and active they must be.

The hunters steadily passed on through the woods. After what seemed hours to Tom they came upon the stretch he had forded on horseback earlier in the fall. He was gratified to see that not near as much water was flowing in the stream bed now as was on the previous occasion. They managed to cross without any difficulty. Then began the ascent

on the opposite side. Very shortly the Indian came

across fresh turkey signs. The birds were working

up the mountainside. Now a noticeable change was

manifested in Debassius. He stole forward through

the young timber and underbrush as noiseless as a

shadow. His long right arm was out thrust to ward

off any limbs of saplings that might be in his path.

His lean raven-haired head was constantly held in

a listening attitude.

In this fashion the flat top of the ridge was

reached. As they quietly crept around the east

clump of laurel just at the edge of the flat,

Debassius instantly raised his right hand to

shoulder level. A warning hiss-s-s came from him.

Tom craned his neck and looked past the Indian,

but strain his eyes as he would he couldn't see a thing that even faintly resembled a wild turkey. Jane smiled at his efforts, and stood quietly watching Jim. He had seen or heard something she knew.

Abruptly the Indian stretched forth a long arm and pointed directly to the fore. In a low silent whisper he informed his companions that wild turkeys were on the flat ahead. He dropped to his hunkers and motioned for them to do likewise. Looking at Tom and Jane a wide grin spread across his usually immobile features. He spoke softly.

"Well podners', there's turkeys ahead," he stated. "I don't know how many, or how big they are, but I seen' them scratchins' way across the flat."

"How're we going to get close enough for a shot at them?" Tom asked. "I looked and looked but I couldn't see a thing. They must be a mile away."

"Are you-all goin' to try and creep up for a shot or are you-all goin' to walk right out an' let them fly up?" Jane inquired.

"Which do you two want me to do?" he asked them. "If we scatter them I'll have to call them back together."

"Scatter them Jim," Jane implored. "I want to hear the racket they make when they go up. An' then it'll be fun to hide an' call up a big wise old gobbler." Tom nodded accent.

Debassius said no more but rose from his squatting position and motioning of them to follow and started across the flat directly toward where he had seen the big birds. They were more than half way across when a low put-putting sound came from ahead. This sound continued for a little while, and directly Tom could see large brownish birds swiftly running through the underbrush some distance ahead, and slightly to their right. They walked on. Here the signs of the turkey's activities were much to be seen. Whole squares of the leaves and leaf mold were scratched up. The floor of the forest in places looked as if a number of hogs had been rooting around. The feathered denizens of this forest land who had created this havoc of

leaves and topsoil apparently had vanished. Not a

sight of them were to be heard or seen.

The Indian and his two companions walked

on across the flat. More than a hundred feet to the

fore appeared a few clumps of the small mountain

laurel. It stood at a height of more than five feet for

even the tallest of the evergreen shrubs. For the

most part the laurel was about a yard in height and

grew in loose formations. Small green leaves about

the size of a man's thumb covered the small

twisted, gnarled evergreens. Their every

appearance bespoke of a great age. Old rotting logs

lay scattered around among the clumps of laurel.

That Debassius made directly for them.

Instinctively he knew where the wild turkeys had

taken cover.

Not a sign of a turkey was seen until they reached the first old log that lay at the edge of the laurel growth. Then it was that Tom thought for a few moments that the forest was crashing down upon their heads. In a flash the air around them seemed full of thundering, crashing birds of huge size, that flew away through the tree-tops in all directions, at incredible speed. One moment not a sight or sound of them did they see. While the next moment with wildly flapping, thundering, beating wings, the large game birds were up and away. Tom and Jane stood transfixed, while the Indian raised both his long arms aloft, and gave vent to his singular yell. In a few seconds all was quiet again. The turkeys had made their departure as swiftly as they had put in an appearance.

Dropping his arms to his sides Jim swung
around and confronted Tom and Jane with a low
laugh. His dark face wore an expression of keenest
enjoyment. His black eyes were alive with a
leaping flame.

"Well now folks," he drawled in his quiet
unhurried way. "Seein' as how they're scattered,
reckon the next thing for us to do is find a good
spot, where we'll be well hid an' start callin'"

"How'll you do that?" Tom asked.

"Daddy says Jim uses a birch bark box for a
call," Jane remarked, and at her words the Indian

took from his jacket pocket a queer looking little flat box like contraption. There were two slits along its sides from which protruded a strip of birch bark. Debassius held the gadget in one hand and grasping the strip of birch bark pulled on it. It slid through the slits. At its' moving a squawking sound was heard. When this occurred Jim raised his eyes from his turkey call and grinned.

"Yes, Tom his little device is a homemade turkey call," he replied. "An' its' never failed me yet. Let's see how it'll work today."

Immediately then he cast his eyes around them for a suitable blind behind which they could hide while he worked his caller. As none satisfactory was to be seen he motioned to his companions and began to walk on across the flat. At about a hundred yards or so from where the turkeys had gone up he found a natural blind. Two old chestnut stumps had sprouts shooting up from their roots to a height of approximately six feet. They were standing close together and within a few feet on one side of them grew a scattered out clump of small mountain laurel. The chestnut sprouts hadn't shed all of their leaves as yet, and afforded excellent shelter behind which to hide. On the other side the laurel screened anyone from view, while within this natural blind a person hiding here could see out very good, without much risk of being seen himself.

Then the hunters were set inside the blind, Debassius began manipulating his birch bark caller. Long drawn-out squawks rose on the still air. These became more inducing as time went on. Jane had told Tom that the sounds made by this little box of bark were amazingly like the call of a hen turkey, and that when heard the old gobblers would answer and come toward the sound. The squawking sound continued. They had become more plaintive. The skillful hands of the Indian sent forth the interesting call, again, and again. Results were soon forth coming. A distinct "Gobble, gobble, gobble," was heard off to the left, and some distance away. Soon an answering "Gobble" was heard to the right, and directly ahead.

The wailing cry continued. And in a moment or so the gobbler to their left answered again. This time he was much closer. Debassius cocked his shot gun and laid it directly before him on the leaves.

The mournful cry sounded again. The answer came this time from quite close by. All eyes were turned to the direction of the approaching gobbler. A faint rustle was heard in the leaves. Then a sight occurred that made Tom's heart give a big leap.

A huge old gobbler had miraculously appeared among the trees about seventy five feet away. One moment he was not there, and the next moment, there he was. He ran a few feet nearer the blind, then all of a sudden he stopped. Up shot his long neck to an extraordinary height. And he swept the surrounding forest with the keenest of eyes. This feathered monarch of the hills was very smart, and had suddenly become suspicious. Things were not as they should be he knew. He craned his long neck in vain, trying to see the hen turkey who had so piteously called to him. But she was nowhere to be seen. He began to step nervously about, jerking his head up and down as he moved.

The old gobbler was a wise old bird. But this day he was destined to become the victim of an advisory endowed with far greater wisdom. At the moment the turkey put in his appearance the Indian quickly laid aside his birch bark box caller, and instantly retrieving his shotgun, thrust the barrel among the leafy branches that formed their camouflage. A brief smile flitted across his dark features. Pressing forward he keenly sighted down the barrel of the gun at the confused gobbler. A moment then he delayed his shot. Jim Debassius was at that moment in his element. A red hunter matching suits with feathered denizens of the forest. Tom was singularly thrilled at the Indians' display of cunning and destructive appearance. But the red hunter was but living true to the age-old craftiness of his ancestors handed down from generation to generation.

Jane watched the scene before her with fascinated gaze. Not a sound did she make, but as one brought up to such things, swung a sharp eye to and fro to see if any more gobblers had responded to the calls Debassius had sent out. A streak of fire shot forth from the muzzle of the gun Jim was holding to his shoulder. A loud booming report instantly followed. At the report of the gun the big gobbler bounded into the air and turned a somersaulting flip-flop backwards. Falling upon the leaves the great bird stretched out his wings and drummed out in a fluttering motion his last few moments of life.

At the fall of the old gobbler once more the Indians wild yell rang through the forest. Ejecting the spent shell from the chamber of his gun he quickly reloaded it with a new one. Giving his usual low laugh, he then spoke in his drawling way.

"One down so far folks. An' I'm hopin'

we've two more to go. We'll wait awhile an' then I'll begin callin' again. Got to give them turkeys time to quit shakin' from the sound of the shot. If we get another one to come in range decide now which one of you'll take a crack at him."

"Let Jane try her luck on the next one," Tom said. "I'll wait for number three. Cause something tells me that'll be the king-pin turkey of the day."

"O.K. Tom," Jane replied. "If that's how you've got it doped out. You-all could be a little off in your calculations you know. Maybe after I pot number two, you'll wait in vain for yours to show up. Start that squawkin' box up again Jim. I'm gettin' anxious to bag the prize turkey of this hunt. I just know he waited for me," and she looked from one to the other of the two men and smiled broadly. They grinned and nodded their heads in return.

The birch box caller was put into operations again. Once more those plaintive cries lifted on the clear cool air. They were sometimes short calls of longing. When the master hand of the Indian would manipulate the bark box in such a way as to make the squawks come forth in long drawn out pleadings. His efforts began to bear fruit. An answer was heard way off to one side. After much coaxing it came again. This calling and answering back and forth went on for a few moments before it became noticeable that the gobbler was approaching the blind. Debassuis whispered to Jane to get set for action. Another call went out, and the "Gobble, gobble, gobble," in answer immediately followed. He was getting very close. A rustling, pattering sound fell on their ears.

All eyes keenly peered in the directions of that sound. A brownish object appeared moving swiftly among the trees off their right about fifty yards away. It was a large turkey gobbler and he was running directly toward them. Running like a horse, with his long neck stretched out and his tail feathers spread. When he came within about a hundred feet of the blind he slowed to a walk. Like his predecessor, he too was suspicious. Slowly the wary bird walked forward. His head darted this way and that, and to the watchers it seemed almost as if he was actually looking behind the trees he passed in his search for the imagined hen turkey.

When the bird was well within shooting range the Indian whispered to the tense girl by his side. With the outward calm of a veteran hunter Jane thrust forward her shot gun and took aim at the quarry. A moment she sighted the flustered, suspicious gobbler, as he was ducking his warbled head about. The instant he became quiet was his last living moment. At the roar of the gun he bounded into the air a full three feet off the ground. Falling back to earth the strong old gobbler rolled and flopped about as death claimed him, at last to fall in quivering, feathered heap, to rise no more.

At the expiration of the second turkey's life, once more Debassius reacted with his wild cry. Tom had come to realize that such expressions were but a living part of the make-up of Jim Debassius. It was born and bred into him to behave in just a manner. All in all it was ancestral cry of victory.

At this second turkey's demise, another round of low-voiced banter took place. The Indian cautioned Tom and Jane against stepping outside their blind, because there might be some sharp eyed gobblers lurking close by. More than two birds had answered the calls made by the bark box, they knew, and might be close by at the moment.

So they remained in seclusion and kidded each other.

"Jane that sure was a right fine little gobbler

you-all just knocked over," Debassius drawled lazily in a low voice.

"That fine little old gobbler'll make yours look puny in comparison Jim Debassius," she flashed back at him instantly. Tom grinned at them and said nothing. He hoped he would get a shot at a gobbler, and bring him down if he was that fortunate.

"If you two are displeased with the fine birds you've just shot, I'll take them off your hands," he told them with a big smile on his face. "Providing that is that you help me carry them back home."

"We'll take them along ourselves," Jane

answered. "Jim here is just scared that gobbler I shot is a bigger one then the one he got. An' to be honest I believe it is."

"O.K.," the Indian said. "When we get back the scales'll tell the story," and with these words he reached for his birch bark caller again. "Now all I want is to coax a nice big fat one out of hiding for Tom. We'll have to be beatin' it back towards home soon. Be dark now by the time we get there."

He squinted at the sun which had begun to swing down towards its setting place. Tom's watch showed two-thirty, and in two hours and a half more it would be about dark. All three quietly ate the last round of their sandwiches. When they had finished, Debassius started using his turkey caller.

This time it was much longer in bringing results. But once a gobbler was enticed to answer he kept it up and began to move towards the place where the hen turkey was sending up her yearning calls. The third gobbler was coaxed out of hiding to his death. The one Tom shot was the smallest of the three, and he laughingly told his companions that he was glad. That way he wouldn't have such a load to carry on the long trail home. Each of the male turkeys had appeared from hiding quickly and unexpectedly. Stretching their long necks and plainly showing that they were suspicious. Only to linger too long in the vicinity of the blind. Their coloring was a dark blackish brown with streaks of white across the tail feathers. All were beautifully marked and very well feathered against the cold long winter which was ready to sweep across the high country. The day had been highly successful, and the homeward trek was made in good spirits by the trio of hunters. Darkness was shutting down fast as they dropped down into the big cove above the Burton residence. The dogs heralded morning, and met them up in the valley in the little bottom by the black walnut tree. The bearded mountaineer was standing in the yard as they come up the little slope to the big cabin.

"Well, well," he boomed out. Looking at each keenly in the dusky light as they approached him. "Home at last I see, an' looks to me as if we'll have roasted turkey a-plenty. By the Good Lord above three nice fat ones. Well I'll be doggoned. Must be lots of turkeys in the woods this season. Wish now I'd gone along, too. But no matter.

Come right on in. Suppers ready an' waitin'. Lucy
said you three would come back loaded. An you
shore did. Haw, Haw."

Wheeling round the big man made for the
kitchen door. He entered to swing it wide and in
his hearty way announced to his wife that Jane and
the boys were home and had brought in the bacon.

Jane strode in proudly and unceremoniously
dropped her turkey on the kitchen floor. Wearily
the girl dropped down upon a chair. She gave her
parents a tired smile and with a gleam in her eyes
waved a hand at Jim and Tom who were also
occupying chairs.

"Oh, I'm most dead," she burst out. "But I

wouldn't have missed this hunt today for nothin'.
We was over on that flat where we cornered the
big bear. A little this side of them rocks. Jim
spotted a flock and we decided to scatter them.
When they went up I thought for a while the
woods was fallin' in. Such a commotion. I almost
jumped out of my skin. Then we found a good
place to hide, an' Jim worked wonders with that
ugly piece of bark he calls his turkey call. He
called them three turkeys out of their hidin' places,
one at a time. Jim shot the first one, I shot the
second, an' Tom waited till last. An' now for the
good news. This one layin' at my feet is the one I
knocked over, an' it is the biggest. Ha ha."

Debassius set slouched down on his chair in
his usual way. A lazy grin spread across his high

cheeked bone face as Jane proclaimed herself to be the owner of the biggest turkey. A pained expression finally replaced the smile when he spoke.

"What a day, what. I'm glad to say we brought home the bacon. But this ungrateful Jane here would let me and Tom starve plum to death while she brags about the elephant of a turkey she brought down. Him an' me packed it almost all the way home for her, or else she'd never have got that old bird out of the woods. Now before we eat I'm for stringing up the scales an' weighin' our respective birds. Wish I had some buck shot to stuff down the throat of mine." He winked broadly at Mr. and Mrs. Burton as he finished his faked complaint about Jane's behavior. Rising painfully from his chair he went over to a small shelf behind the kitchen stove and picked from off it a pair of spring scales. Soon the three birds had been weighed. Jane's weighed twenty-six pounds. Jim's weighed twenty-four pounds and Tom's was a nice fat twenty pounds. Tired as she was Jane was jubilant. Debassius congratulated her and promised that if he ever permitted her to go on another turkey hunt with him she would be compelled to do her own calling. He grimaced down at the happy girl as he made this statement. Tom and her parents burst out laughing.

"What do you say to that Jane?" they inquired.

"Fine an' dandy," she replied in her flashing

way. "Meanwhile I'll practice up on getting squawks out of a birch bark contraption, an'll be ready for next time."

"Come on out an' eat everybody, or the food'll get cold," Mrs. Burton instructed. "Dad tell the hunters what you promised someone today down at Mingo."

Everyone found places around the food laden supper table and were soon busy eating. Lige Burton ate in silence for a little while, then looking up from his place made known what commitment he had made that day.

"Haw! Haw! Shore' now an' you-all are goin' to hate me," he began. "It was this way. I was haulin' a few props into Mingo an' happened to meet Preacher Kane. Well to make it short an' sweet I told him you three had gone turkey huntin' today an' if you brought home more than one maybe I could talk you-all into givin' him one. There it is. That's how I stuck out my neck. So what's the verdict?" When he had finished talking Burton sat back in his chair, and chuckling deep in his beard looked at all three in turn with a twinkle in his coal black eyes.

"Well Lige, I think that was right fine of you-all," the Indian replied. "Shore' there's nothin' like a little self-sacrifice to make one feel good. Makes us feel as if we're thinkin' of the other person too instead of ourselves all the time."

"I feel the same way Jim," Jane put in. "A generous hearted gesture is good for one's soul."

"It makes me powerful happy to hear you-all say that Janie girl." Debassius continued. "So now what do you-all say to givin' Silas Kane the turkey you shot? That would please the old fellow to no end."

Jane instantly seen the trap the Indian had led her into. But being too smart to show any outward signs she unhesitatingly volunteered to do so. Jim appeared crestfallen. He had expected a rousing argument. But since none was forthcoming he turned to Tom to see how he looked at the matter.

"I think that's very openhearted of Jane to want to give up the fine bird she bagged today. My personal opinion is this. Let's keep the big turkey and give Preacher Kane the one I shot. It weighs twenty pounds and if I do say so myself that's not a turkey to be sneezed at. He and his wife'll get plenty of wild turkey to eat off that nice fat one."

Mr. and Mrs. Burton had set in silence during the talk about who would consider giving away the turkey he or she had shot. Jim said he would take his bird to the preacher in the morning, because he said, he had been on plenty of turkey hunts before and had brought down many a fine bird. Eventually, it was decided that Jim would give his turkey to Preacher Kane, and Tom said he thought it would be a nice gesture for him to present Doctor and Mrs. Adams with the twenty pound one he had shot. Jane's bird was to remain at the Burton residence. A twenty-six pound one was plenty big enough to supply meat a plenty for all five of them to eat. The following week was Thanksgiving Day. Packed in ice the bird would keep till then.

When supper was over Burton rose from the table and stepped to the kitchen door. Opening it he looked outside into the night. A wind had risen. A cold gust of air swept into the kitchen from the open door. Closing the door the bearded giant repaired to the side of the cook stove and sank down upon a low stool.

"Shore' an' you-all just got your turkey

huntin' done in the nick of time," he rambled. "It's clouded over tight, an' is snowin'. Already the yard is white. Might get up in the mornin' an' find a feet or two of that white stuff on the ground. Right time now to expect it anytime."

"Mr. Burton," Tom inquired. "How deep a snow have you ever seen in this high country at one time?"

"Well now son as I recollect, I've seen more than one snow fall that measured close to four feet on a level." Came the answer, "Howsoever, snows like that are not as the ordinary rule. You-all can expect, an' get, plenty of two foot snows right along."

"When the real big ones come what do you do?"

"Nothin', exceptin' to get plenty of fire wood in an' see that the stock is well fed an' have open water to drink."

"It gets plenty cold here in the wintertime, Tom," Jane informed him. "Last winter it was way down below zero several times."

"This comin' winter Jane you-all will be snug an' warm with your new scarf wrapped round your neck an' your new gloves on," drawled the Indian.

"You won't be so bad off yourself with your

new shirts on," she came back with. "Daddy and Mother always bundle up and keep warm, but how're you-all goin' to keep from freezin' in real cold weather Tom. You're not used to this high country winters and might as well look forward to a chilly time ahead."

"I'll put on the heavy longhandles that I bought in Valley Head yesterday," Tom replied. "And if it gets too cold, well I can maybe set in the house by the fireside. We'll wait and see."

They sat in the kitchen and talked for an hour or so longer, before retiring for the night. The dishes were washed and put into the cupboard. Burton and his Indian employee sat and smoked their pipes. Jane coaxed Tom into another round of

Checkers. This time they both won a game. Mrs. Burton sat by the table and worked on a rag rug she was making.

Debassius was first to rise and excuse himself for the night. Mr. and Mrs. Burton soon retired afterwards. Tom and Jane sat and warred back and forth on the third checker game. Soon as they were alone the brown eyed girl's interest in the game they were playing seemed to vanish. Without any explanation for her actions, she quietly laid the board and checkers aside. In a moment she was in his arms. Her arms around him, her lips turned up to receive his. Few words were spoken between them, for words were not necessary to impart their feelings for each other.

At last good night was spoken slowly, and lovingly. A last lingering kiss was shared. A last long look was looked into each other's eyes. Tom stepped outside into the snow-covered yard. A good two inches had fallen. Winter was shutting down over the mountains. He thoughtfully crossed to the cabin he shared with the singular Indian, and soon had undressed and retired for the night; his heart full to overflowing with the storm of his love for Jane Burton.

The long winter months slowly passed. During good weather when there wasn't too much snow on the ground, Tom and Jim continued to cut mine props. When the snows were drifted deep all the men of the Burton household did was cut firewood and see that the stock was well cared for.

That in itself was no small task. As Lige Burton

had told him in November of the deep snows that

sometimes fell on high country, Tom saw one of

these drifters in January of that winter.

Christmas time had come and gone

uneventfully, save for the usual Yuletide activities

that prevail in a rural community. Gifts galore were

given back and forth in the Burton home. Jane and

Tom went on walks on some of the clear cold

winter evenings. The mountain girl had seemed to

retreat into herself as the winter wore on. A

haunting look had crept into the back of her

beautiful clear brown eyes. Instinctively Tom knew

what was on the mind of the girl he loved, but for

the present he could not bring himself to speak. He

looked forward longingly to the coming springtime

wherein he had a certain conviction momentous things were going to happen. He felt in his heart that at that time somehow the mystery that shrouded the night riding of Lige Burton and Jim Debassius would be explained. Somehow he knew that with the coming of good weather again they would be out and on the go on certain nights till long after midnight. And he was determined to know where they went and what they did on these night trips.

January was drawing to a close when the big storm that, brought the deep snows, swept over the mountain countryside. All day it had been trying to add more snow to the four or five inches remaining on the terrain from the last snowfall. Long in the afternoon the sky off to the northwest began to push up the big black clouds. A low moaning sound came on the keen knife-like wind that had begun to blow. The light snowflakes that had been lazily falling out of the gray clouds all day were soon replaced by very large fluffy ones that rode on the wind like big downy feathers.

As the afternoon wore on the storm grew steadily worse. The stock was cared for early that evening. Water ponds were cut free of ice and the horses and cattle and sheep drank their fill. A generous supply of firewood was stacked up at both cabins. By nightfall over half a foot was on the level land and already on the slopes it had begun to drift. When full night had shut down, the storm increased its fury. It began to snow much heavier. Once when Burton opened the kitchen door to look outside a thrilling sight met the eyes of those at the supper table. The force of the storm had increased to a high whining sound. This in turn gave way to an awesome crashing roar. The storm was sweeping over the cabin in a frightful manner. A whirling white pile of snow was seen outside the open door. Hundreds of huge flakes came floating into the kitchen. The mountaineer shut the heavy door with a slam and strode back to the dinner table.

"Shore' an' it's one helluva night out there," he boomed in his hearty way. "I'd hate to be out in that. Don't think I've ever seen it snow harder. Boys you'll shore' have to swing shovels tomorrow mornin'. If this keeps up all night, there'll be better'n three feet on the level. Looks like one of them old fashioned snows I told you-all about last fall Tom. Mother pour me another cup of hot coffee. That trip to the door sort of put a chill in my old bones. Haw, haw."

Everybody laughed at this last remark. Supper was finished and soon the dishes were washed and dried and put back in their usual places. A roaring fire was built in the big living room fireplace. All agreed to set up till after midnight to see how the storm acted. Maybe it would blow itself out in an hour or so. Then again maybe it was set to roll along for many hours to come. One could never tell about those mountain storms.

Deer heads hung around the walls of the

huge living room. Several bear skin rugs lay on the floor. In the center of the floor lay a big round black bear skin. A small table set in the center of it. Upon which lay a number of books and magazines. A large family Bible was in evidence. Seeing Tom looking at the big black bearskin Burton and the Indian gave a chuckle.

"Does that hide look familiar?" they asked.

"I'm not sure, but seems I've seen that black pelt before," he answered.

"Well son that came off that old sheep killer we did for last fall way over on that ridge among them rocks," Burton informed him. "Jane insisted Jim tan it for her, an' so there it lays before you-all."

"That's my favorite bearskin rug," Jane said softly. "I'll never forget that hunt, an' what a terrific fight that old devil put up. He was as awful an' wild an' fierce as they come."

"That was sure a hunt to remember, Janie girl." Tom agreed. "If he was alive tonight I'll bet he would be holed up back in that big laurel bed somewhere. I'd like to see that place with all the snow this storm will drop on it. It'll probably be covered up."

"I was back up there four years ago when there was a two foot and a half snow on that had crusted," Debassius told him. "It was shore' purty.

All humpy an' lumpy with snow an' with some of

the scattered tall laurel trees sticking up out of the

snow with their long green leaves shinin' in the

sun. I seen several holes made into the big bed

where bears had come out into the sun to stretch

some an' then gone back in. They do that

sometimes, on warm days, in the middle of the

winter."

The men folks talked for hours and

occasionally fed the roaring fire in the big

fireplace. It hissed and snapped as the flakes of

snow fell into it from down the chimney. Before

midnight Jane and her mother retired for the night.

The mountaineer followed them to his bed in less

than an hour. Tom and Jim said they would sleep

on the floor before the open fire for the remainder

of the night.

The storm raged on and on through the long hours. The wind howled and moaned round the strong long structure. At times, it would sound its voice in a low sweeping roar. Sharp gusts would slap against the log walls with amazing force. Then the cabin would tremble and vibrate. A dwelling of lesser strength would have been battered badly. Occasionally the voice of the storm would cry out in shrieking crescendo, to diminish in long wails that sounded not unlike a legion of demons loose in the night. A pinching cold began to creep into the huge living room. The Indian looked at Tom and drawled that zero weather would follow the storm. The kitchen door was opened no more.

The two men slept but fitfully on the hard floor. They were unused to such a bed, but had promised to keep the fire going. Morning came at last. Cold and gray and with still a whirling shroud of snow tumbling down. The force of the storm had abated considerably, but the flakes were dropping thick as ever. A world of white greeted the gaze of the occupants of the big cabin.

When Burton had eaten his breakfast, he stepped to the kitchen door, and throwing back the bar, opened it about half way. An eighteen-inch wall of snow stood on the door step, and stretched out across the yard in an uneven broken blanket. At the corner of the room Tom had made his recovery in, a huge pile of white snow and curved away like a sand dune.

"Great Day in the mornin'," rolled out Burton in his sonorous voice. "Look at that snow. Its' two feet from the level of the yard to the door step, an' there's a foot an' a half of snow above the step. I'll say right now we've got better'n a three-footer on a level out there. An' it's still snowin'. We'll have one helluva time getting paths shoveled to the barn an' other places. But we've gotta' do it."

As Burton had stated the snow lay a good forty inches deep on level ground. Where it was drifted the blanket was much heavier. Toward noon the storm blew itself out and in an hour afterwards, the clouds broke and the sun broke through in dazzling rays for a few minutes. The rift closed in the heavens and the sun was lost to view. But for

the present the snow had ceased to fall. A

tremendous amount of snow had fallen over the

high country. It stretched up the valley, and

climbed the mountain slopes on both sides of the

creek, in an unbroken covering of white. The

pathways the three men shoveled looked like deep

ditches. The stock was fed and led to water in the

afternoon. All day they toiled. When nighttime was

shutting down in the evening the air had taken on a

piercing quality. It began to clear off and stars

came into view to twinkle and blaze in the still

cold atmosphere. That evening Tom and Jim had

built a fire in the fireplace in the cabin they shared.

They retired early while the room their beds were

in was nice and warm. All along through the night

one or the other of them would get out of bed, and

replenish the fire. By the creeping bite of the cold Tom was convinced it was intensely cold outside. Next morning the thermometer outside their door stood at fifteen below zero. Tom laughed when Debassius put on two heavy shirts, and overalls on over his work pants. But the Indian only smiled and refused to talk about his mode of dressing for cold weather. After he had eaten his breakfast Tom started into doing the chores. The bite of the cold was very penetrating. Before the chores were half done he seen the wisdom of the Indian's dressing for such weather. Debassius went about his work with his usual calm easy air. Occasionally he would briskly rub his ears. Tom finally froze out and had to go to the house to warm up. When he went past their cabin he glanced at the thermometer and was amazed to see it had dropped three more degrees. It now stood at eighteen below zero. Shivering, the revenue man walked on.

The bitter cold was wide spread. Reports came into the little town of Mingo as the days passed of the temperature readings in other sections of the Nation. For two weeks it was below zero every night. The coldest morning the mercury slid down to a bone chilling twenty-five below. That day the warmed it got was five below. In another week the weather began to moderate. The big snow began to crust at night. Finally, it had settled down to two feet. More fell on it, another cold spell, but not so many sub-zero nights as before. February slowly passed into March. The big snow had fallen in January and it was still plenty deep even after six weeks had elapsed. It disappeared in a lazy, reluctant fashion. The big drifts lasted the longest, up the hills and in low depressions and wherever the howling wind had chosen to play freakish tricks. There one would find the long curving mounds. April was near at hand when with three days and nights of steady foggy rainy weather, the snow faded completely away.

Soon as possible after the big deluge of snow Tom and Jim resumed their prop cutting. They cut and trimmed the long slender trees and left them where they lay to later haul away to cut and split to the splitting yard later once the snow had sufficiently settled.

By the time winter had passed into spring

the two men had an enormous pile of props cut and split and ready to haul down to Mingo. Burton had decreed that by the time they could get delivered what they had cut, it would be crop time. All through most of April they hauled props. As the sun grew more direct in its shining, the roads and countryside gradually lost their sponginess. The last week of April found the road to Mingo quite dry and well packed. When the buyer of the props and Lige Burton took a final count of all props that had been cut and delivered, Tom was amazed and delighted to know that he and Debassius had cut and split more than fifteen thousand. All in all a tidy sum of money was realized form their winters work.

"Shore' now boys," the heavy voice of the

mountaineer rolled out. "I'm more'n pleased with the results. An' I'm givin' you both a crisp new twenty dollar bill to show it. Reckon as how I'll have to slip Janie girl a ten spot to keep her off my neck. An' maybe more'n that before I'm through shellin' out. She told me recent she wants to buy a couple of new dresses an' other things this spring, so I'm preparin' myself to get robbed. May was in its third week before the high country had completely clothed itself in green again. The deep coves and high ragged ridges and sharp prominaries were not the most laggard. And with the coming of good weather, the giant mountaineer and his Indian employee once again resumed their night-time activities. Jane and her mother put up a gallant front of pretending nothing was troubling them, but to the trained eyes of the revenue man;

their pretense was as clear as an inch of crystal water.

Lige Burton's outward appearance remained much the same. Only his coal black eyes told the tale. Into their depths had crept a steely glint which seemed wont to burst into flame at the slightest provocation.

Debassius continued to be unreadable as ever. How cool, and slow, and easy he was. With his lazy drawling speech and quiet good natural way. Of the two men Tom knew he would much rather face the raging wrath of the mountaineer then the ice deadliness of the Indian. When such thoughts came, he prayed that the day might never come wherein he would be called upon to face their anger.

With the coming of the warm sunny days of June, a marked change was introduced into the mysterious doings of Burton and his singular companion. Abruptly they discontinued their night-riding. This occurred immediately upon their return from an absence of two days and nights. There after Tom would be awakened long in the night by the Indian entering the cabin they shared. Silently he would slip out of bed and away, and just as silent and stealthy would be the Red man's return.

When the significance of this dawned upon Tom, a rippling thrill traveled the entire length of his body. Such a change in their activities could mean but one thing. Whatever they had done on their night-time trips, they were now doubtless doing near at hand, and within walking distance. The time he had looked forward to, and had dreaded had finally come. At the first opportune time, he resolved to follow the Indian when he slipped out of bed and vanished into the night.

June was two-thirds gone before the night came. He had retired early that evening. All day he had been repairing the drift fence the mountaineer had strung along the crest of the long ridge above the big cove. Four strangles of four point barbed wire had been stretched from sapling to sapling in an uneven zigzag manner out the ridge for more than two miles. At either end of their fence it curve down onto lower ground to intermingle with other fences. The purpose of this ridge fence was to keep whatever stock that was grazing in the huge cove pasture field from wandering over the ridge and down into the endless tract of woods that lay beyond. Years of experience in mountain grazing had taught the stockmen of that high country that such a fence was invaluable. Sheep and lambs and young calves were easy victims of bears, bob cats, and panthers, when the stock was allowed to roam deep into the woods.

Tom fell asleep soon after retiring. He was barely aware of the Indian coming to bed. By the light of the lantern, the clock on the chair at the head of his bed showed nine-thirty. Hours later he was awakened by the noise of someone moving around in the other room. Laying quietly he listened intently. There came a sound as if someone bumped into the bed or a chair in the darkness. A low muttered curse instantly followed. Thrillingly Tom recognized Jim Debassius as the owner of that voice. The Indian was preparing to slip away into the night on another of his mysterious trips. And this time the revenue man was determined to follow him.

Debassius came slipping quietly towards the room where Tom lay. Tom heard him stop to listen as he reached the door, and he purposely made his breathing slow and deep to deceive the listening Red man. Apparently satisfied, the door opened noiselessly and the Indian glided like a shadow into the night. The door closed softly behind his tall dark form.

A few seconds later the revenue man stole quietly from his bed and cautiously approached the window. Standing a safe distance back from the panes, he intently peered out into the night. A low moon shed its' uncertain light down into the mountain valley. The window through which the revenue man was looking faced upstream and toward the barn. A well-used path led from the Burton home up the valley. Dimly he could see the tall slim figure of the Indian striding along the path, heading upstream. As Tom watched, the form of Debassius became fainter and fainter in the tricky moonlight until soon he was lost to view. Not a sound did the three hounds make as the Indian left the two-room cabin and stalked off into the night. Tom hoped he would raise no sound from them when he took the trail behind

Debassius. Hurriedly he dressed in the darkness

and cautiously opening the door stepped out.

Quietly closing it behind him he soon was walking

swiftly along the path that led up the valley. He

would have to be very careful, as he well knew the

man he was trailing had the eyes of a hawk, and

very sharp ears. Consequently, he moved as quietly

as possible.

The weeds that bordered the path was wet

with dew. How late it was he didn't know. He was

leery of risking a light to see the clock before he

left the cabin. He guessed it to be close to midnight

or a little later.

Night sounds were all around him as he

moved rapidly along the trail. Frogs were softly croaking in the little stream. Crickets were making a merry bedlam. Night birds were making themselves heard. Hoot owls were hooting back in the timber on the ridges to either side of the mountain valley. The haunting and lonely cry of the whip-poor-will sounded across in the big cove, and up the slopes.

When Tom rounded the bend in the creek below, at the big double black walnut tree, he moved with extreme caution. He was thrilled to see Debassius ahead in the dim moonlight turn to the right after passing the big tree and crossing the small valley begin to climb a gently sloping point that came down to the valley floor. He remembered that the winter before he had noticed an old path climbing the crest of this point and going back into the woods. Where this path led, he knew not because he had never followed it.

Waiting until the Indian had disappeared in the second growth timber on the point, he then hurriedly crossed the valley and began the gradual ascent. The old path was fairly easy to follow, and once the timber was reached it seemed to have a natural lane through the underbrush.

The moon shining down through the trees made ghostly shadows all along the trail. Up and up climbed the path, and the way began to be considerably steeper. The terrain commenced to be dotted with rocks of generous size. They loomed up in the pale moonlight; dark, shadowy, and uninviting. The trail led straight up over what must have been an outcropping ledge. After this steep ascent was made, it took a sharp swing to the left round a shoulder that jutted out. Abruptly Tom froze in his tracks. He had caught the sound of low voices coming on the night air from directly ahead. He stood perfectly still for a few moments, then softly stole along the path toward the sound of those voices. A peculiar odor came to his nostrils on the soft night breeze. The pale glow of a fire was seen. A curve in the trail abruptly halted his stealthy approach. The glow of the fire came from a small cove-like depression. The murmur of running water was heard coming from that direction. Doubtless it was made by the rushing waters of a mountain spring.

Here at the bend in the trail, Tom could plainly smell the odor he had noticed a moment before. It hung heavy in the air, and was of a hot, whiskey-like nature. Instantly the revenue man knew what that peculiar scent meant. He had smelled that odor before. It came from a distill, and one that was in operation distilling mash to make whiskey. A hissing, bubbling sound came from the cove-like depression. Quickly taking in the scene before him with a few razor-sharp glances, Tom glided to the side of the trail and crouched down behind a rock. The night was warm and he sent a silent prayer up to the starry sky above that there would be no snakes within striking distance. Since his near fatal experience the summer before, he had been told by more than one of these mountain people that rattlesnakes very seldom was abroad after nightfall and they were practically the only poisonous snake in that section.

From his position behind the rock, Tom had only to glance around the edge to get a good view of what was going on in the little cove ahead. A sweat broke out all over his body. For a little while he shook as one afflicted with the ague. This night he was witnessing that which he had come into this mountain country to stop. A whiskey distill was going full blast directly in front of him. And its' owners and operators were seated around it. His senses were keenly alert as the revenue man raised his head and with a sharp eye and ear looked round the edge of the rock at the distill and its' attendants. The voices of the men came distinctly to his ears.

A glowing fire was burning in the little cove.
Over it was mounted a long dark tank of some sort.
From the top of this tank a slender tube of metal
rose to curve and disappear on the opposite side.
The bubbling, boiling and hissing sound was much
in evidence. To one side of the fire, a dark figure
was busy dipping something liquid out of a barrel
and straining it through a cloth tied across the top
of a sizeable container. Tom knew at once what the
man was doing. He was straining the grain out of
the whiskey mash before distilling it.

The men set in a semi-circle around the fire.
Its' flickering light played on their dark shadowy
faces. Most of them were smoking. One of them

rose from his seat and went to where the murmuring water was running. Bending down he took a tin cup and dipping up the running water poured it into something that stood by his side. He kept this up for several moments. At last, apparently satisfied, the man walked back to his seat and sat down. Something vaguely familiar about the man caused Tom to keenly watch him. When he spoke it was with a shock that he recognized him. It was Sam Davis. The first man he had spent the night with last summer when he dropped over into the Cheat River Country. Just then Davis spoke.

"Well, now, Indian Jim," came the man's bluff hearty voice. "I see you-all got here on time, but where in hell is the boss? Last time I seen him, he promised me faithful he'd show up tonight."

"Sam," the cool, easy drawl of Debassius replied. "Take it easy, an' I believe you'll be talkin' to the boss, an' very soon."

The Indian sat slouched down on his seat in his usual way. The flickering flames of the fire played softly on his dark hawk like features. Rising from his seat he threw quite a few sticks of wood on the fire. It blazed up brightly. By the better light it afforded, Tom studied the man he had not recognized before. To one side set a white haired mountaineer. He was silently puffing on a short stemmed pipe. When he spoke it was also his voice that betrayed him to the revenue man.

"Sam how's the old still puttin' out tonight?" the man asked in a pleasant cordial way. He was Brown, whom Tom had spent a night with last summer. So he and Davis were both moonshiners underneath their appearance of being just farmers and timber cutters. It was a good eighty miles to Davis's home from where he set, and Tom honestly was at a loss to know what was he doing way over here sitting by the side of a distill, and in the middle of the night. Four other men set round the fire, but they were silent. One of the four then spoke to Debassius.

"Shore' hope the boss'll get here soon. I don't like this place for our Stillwell. Too hard to get to. But maybe it's best that way. Not likely to be much danger of a revenue man snoopin' around up here. That's one nice thing about this spot. And another thing we've plenty of good, cool water here to put the coil in. But I still ain't in love with this God-forsaken place."

"Well now, Luke," drawled the Indian. "I know this spot ain't no good side park for getting to but the way I see it, that's all the better. Last summer we near got caught a couple of times cause we were close to the road. An' them outside fellers that are in these hills lookin' for us would like nothing' better'n to salt this whole gang away. An' for a good long spell."

"Me, I'm for stayin' on the safe side much as possible," spoke up one of the men round the fire that Tom didn't know.

"We'll put it up to the boss when he gits' here, about movin' our still that is," said another.

"Sam, how much are we boilin' off tonight?" asked the mountaineer Brown again.

"Reckon near as I can figure, we'll sack off close to twenty-five gallons, an' what with the price of liquor as it is today, it'll bring in a nice slice of jack when we sell it."

"Davis, how long have you-all been familiar with makin' shine liquor?" asked one of the men.

"I recollect my grandfather makin' it, an' he told me fore' he died that liquor makin' had always been in our family. An' the way I look at is if that was good enough for my kinfolk's way back to do, it's good enough for me. But try an' tell them damn revenue men that."

At mention of revenue men, the dark figures round the fire stirred uncomfortable. The following to all family customs in this mountain country didn't interest the revenue men in the slightest. In the city for the sons to follow in the father's footsteps was perfectly all right, but not here in this high country. And that fact rambled deep in the hearts of the down to earth people of the mountains. They didn't give a tinker's damn how the people of the big cities made their living long as they didn't steal or cheat. So they saw it in this light. We'll let you alone. So please let us alone in return. That was their philosophy.

The distill continued to bubble and hiss as time went one. And every now and then as time went on and every now and then one of the gang would throw a few sticks of wood on the fire. A fresh amount of water would be poured into the container that held the copper tubing. Every few minutes this would be done by one of the men.

The semi-circle of men talked and talked as they set waiting for the boss and no two of them had the same opinion. Tom listened with wide open ears. He was very curious to know the identity of this mysterious boss. This was the Cheat Brew gang of that he was certain. The gang of men he had been sent into this country to apprehend.

He stood listening to the sounds of the night around him. The hooting owls, the mournful cry of the whip-poor-will, and the multitude of night bugs and other insects. In the course of time a new sound was heard coming down the trail. It was a long low whistle. When it came for the first time on the night air, the men looked at one another and grinned. Tom was electrified. At last he was going to see the boss. At the whistle one of the men dropped his pipe into his palm and rising from his seat, stepped forth full into the light from the fire.

"That's the boss comin," he said in ringing voice. Soon Tom heard footsteps approaching on the trail behind him. He crouched down close beside the rock behind which he was hiding and looked intently out to the trail. Soon a tall figure came striding into view. In the uncertain light, Tom was positive that the man was not a stranger to him. But if what he suspected was true, then he sincerely hoped this tall boss that was just arriving, was a stranger. The dark figure strode past his hiding place, and on toward the fire. At the edge of the circle of firelight, he paused to cast a sweeping glance around. Then he stopped full into the firelight, and Tom gave an inward exclamation of surprise. There could not be mistaking that man anymore. The tall robust figure, the flashing black eyes, and the heavy beard that was black as night. The man was Lige Burton, and at that moment all the waiting men round the fire hailed him cordially.

"Howdy boss," they chorused.

"Evenin' men," Burton replied. "Shore' an' I hope I've not kept you-all waitin' too long. Was talkin' to the family an' one thing an' another. Howdy there, Sam Davis, you old moonshiner. How's the old kettle percolatin' tonight?"

"Fair to middlin', Lige old boss," Davis answered with a low laugh. "Good cool spring here an' plenty of wood, an' plenty of coves. Way back from the road too, but still part of the gang ain't what you'd call calmly serene. They claim we've sort of buried ourselves in the hills this time. Luke Dawson there says' this place is an' out of the way God forsaken place. Personal, I'm for stayin' in an' out of the way place myself. Lately we've been too close to the beatin' trail, an' came close to lookin' down the long arm of the law a couple of times. The gang want to know your opinion of our present location."

Tom Bell listened and watched Sam Davis and Lige Burton quite closely as they talked. The setup was clear to see. Burton was the boss or leader of the gang, and no doubt Davis was his right hand man. Brown and the others remained in the background. The taciturn Debassius sat in his customary way. Slouched down, with his shadowy face dark and brooding. As Davis put his query up to their leader, the big man seemed to square off as if expecting a hot argument. Slowly he faced each in turn, thoughtfully stroking his heavy beard the while. And as he turned this way and that while facing his men, his big eyes took on a phosphorescent gleam. When he spoke his words carried the weight of careful thought and long meditation. His voice was a low deep rumble. "Men reckon' as how we've all a right to our private opinion as to the spot where we'll set up our still from time to time. An' that's how it should be. But when you-all chose me to be your leader, I took the job reluctantly. Knowin' the hot arguments that would fall round my head. So, now as to my private opinion of this spot here, I suggested this spring on my land because it's a good three miles for any traveled road. And from what's been happenin' up an' down in the high hills the past year or two, the harder our stills is to get at, the longer we'll stay in business, an' the longer we'll stay out of jail. Times have changed. I remember when I was a young feller that a person could make all the moonshine he wanted to an' nobody'd say a word. But not anymore. Then here's another thing. This gang has got ambitions. We talked it over when we went in together that we'd make whiskey to sell only to people who live in the mountains. That has been an old mountain custom to do that. But damn it to hell, the dollar sign has got into some of your eyes an' you're forever pesterin' hell outta' me to branch out an' find a more profitable market for our mountain dew. An' I keep tellin' every man jack of you that when we start that it's the beginnin' of the end. An' some of us'll wind up lookin' through the bars. I hate them damn pesterin' revenue ginks. But just hatin' them won't solve our problem. They're still on our necks, an' believe me they mean big. I heard in Valley Head the other day that a gang of fellows down on the Gauley had been caught an' sent up for a year in the pen. Every one of them. The thought of that ain't a bit attractive to me. So men, a last word before I hear what you-all think of what I've just told you. I've always been a law abidin' man. An' I've my wife and gal to think of too. Makin' mountain liqueur ain't what it once was. Now we're no better'en outlaws in the eyes of the law. I for one don't like it a little bit, an' I'm for breakin' up the gang. Let's quit this business before it backfires in our faces. It ain't as if anyone of us has to depend on what we make out of this to live. I've thought it all out an' that's my decision. How does it strike you?"

At the last few sentences of Lige Burton's speech to his men, Tom was amazed and strangely touched. This stalwart mountaineer who had been chosen as their leader was not on this job in spirit. Tom knew that what he had heard the boss of the Cheat River Gang tell his men confidently, was something Burton would likely never confide to an outsider. The love of the old customs, and the practice of the same. The deep regard for his men, and their welfare. The contempt and animosity toward all those that would infringe on the inherited rights of the people of the high country. His anger and sorrow at having to chastise his men for their reckless and dangerous money making ambitions. The deep regret of the men at the knowledge that they were now considered as almost outlaws. That had been the final word the bearded giant had handed them. Break up the gang, disband, and be no more. Breathlessly, the revenue man waited for the men to break the complete silence that had followed at Burton's disclosure of his decision. Looking at the man standing then before him, with folded arms, and calm unruffled manner, Tom could not but feel a great admiration for Lige Burton as an honest, straight shooting person. He had seen the handwriting on the wall, and had accepted it.

Sam Davis was the first to break the deep silence. A smile was on the face of the man as he rose from his seat before the fire and striding forward grasped the hand of his leader and shook it warmly.

"Boss, I'm shore' gonna' hate not havin'
these get-together to look forward to, but I can see
the wisdom in what you've just told us. The old
days are gone forever an' we'll be wise men to see
that. I also say stop now, before we bring sorrow
and disgrace to our families. Men, I agree with the
boss, let's break up."

At the words of Sam Davis, another of the
group round the fire rose and sanctioned their
decision. It was the white haired mountaineer
farmer Brown. All Jim Debassius was to look up at
the three standing before him, nod his head in
agreement, and casually wave a hand. As usual the
Indian was his lazy, cool, and calm self. Tom had
never seen anything happen since he had made
Debassius acquaintance that had seemed to bother

the man in the slightest. But Tom knew that
underneath the calm outward appearance of the tall
lean Redman, Jim Debassius on occasion could be
as true as a coiled spring, and could move with
lighting speed.

Of the eight men in the gang, four were for
disbanding. The others were the four whom Tom
had never met personally. They set with bowed
heads. Finally the one who earlier in the night had
been addressed as Luke Dawson rose and spoke in
a querulous tone of voice. "We ain't goin' sayin'
the truth in what you've told us tonight boss, but as
spokesman for us other four fellows, we feel that
it's a hasty an' needless decision you're voicin' to
the gang. We say keep on as before, an' if worse
comes to the worse, we can always stop them.

That's the way we feel."

A hot argument ensured, during which Burton stood calmly by and looked on. Davis and Brown finally gave up in disgust. Debassius smiled his dark smile and said nothing. The distill was opened and refilled. A cloud of steam rose when the valve was opened to put the new mash in. Fresh water was put around the copper coil. The fire was built up again. They were ready to run off another batch. Tom had seen and heard enough. He didn't wait to hear the final decision of the gangs would be. As noiseless as a shadow, he stole back into the path, took one last look at the flickering fire. Listened once more to the murmuring spring, and the bubbling hissing distill. Then turning around he silently slipped along the trail back the way he had come. When he rounded the sharp curve, and had made the descent off the steep section of the slope, he began to walk swiftly. Behind him on the mountain, he had just left the Cheat River Gang. He knew who they were now. He had learned their identity. His mission into his mountain country had been in a measure successful. He had come to deeply respect the people of the mountains, and their ways and customs. And tonight he had had his eyes opened.

A thousand thoughts were racing through his head as he walked along. He now knew why Jane and her mother sometimes wore a strained look when Lige Burton and the Indian were away on this sort of business. And his heart went out to them.

He crossed the little bottom of the big walnut tree and in a few minutes was silently climbing the path up to the two roomed cabin. The big cabin sat dark and still. Not a dog put in an appearance. For that he was thankful. Slipping quietly back into the cabin, he soon undressed and crept into bed. Before going to sleep, Tom decided to go and have a long heart to heart, man to man talk with Preacher Kane in the very near future.

To Be Continued in…

Mountain Dew Trilogy III:

Nell's Sojourn

Janice Blanton 2010

Daughter of Nell

Janice Blanton

2-18-2009

Janice and Robert F. Burkhardt

4-5-2016

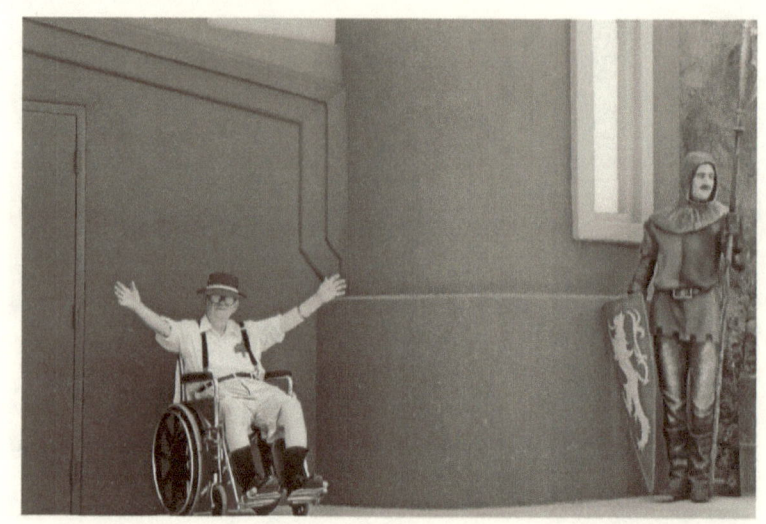

1994-Harold in Vegas

Harold's 84th Birthday

12-23-1997

Harold at the fireplace in their Bay Village Home

1994

1993-Harold gets his GED

January 16, 1992 - Janice and Harold on her 37th Birthday

Early 1960's - Jane and Harold

Harold and daughter, Nancy

Christmas and their Birthdays

1969

Harold H. Milton

1980's-Harold and Janice in the woods

Fall 1969-Nancy, Janice, and Harold at the park

1979-Janice and Harold, his first dance

Harold with his GED

Janice with Harold on his 81st Birthday

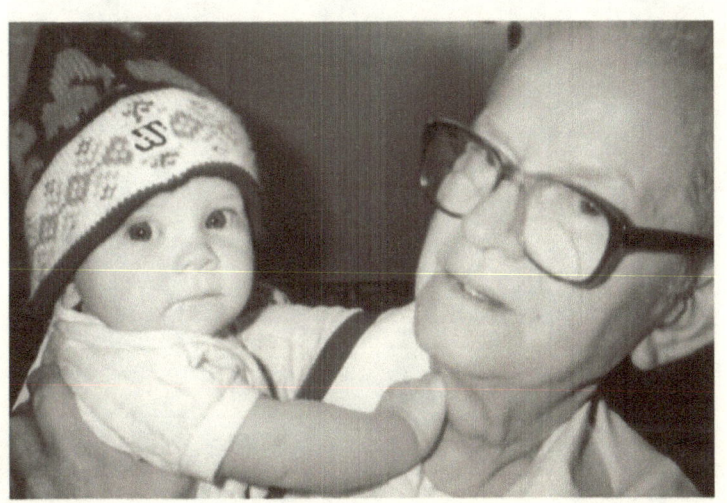

Harold and Madison

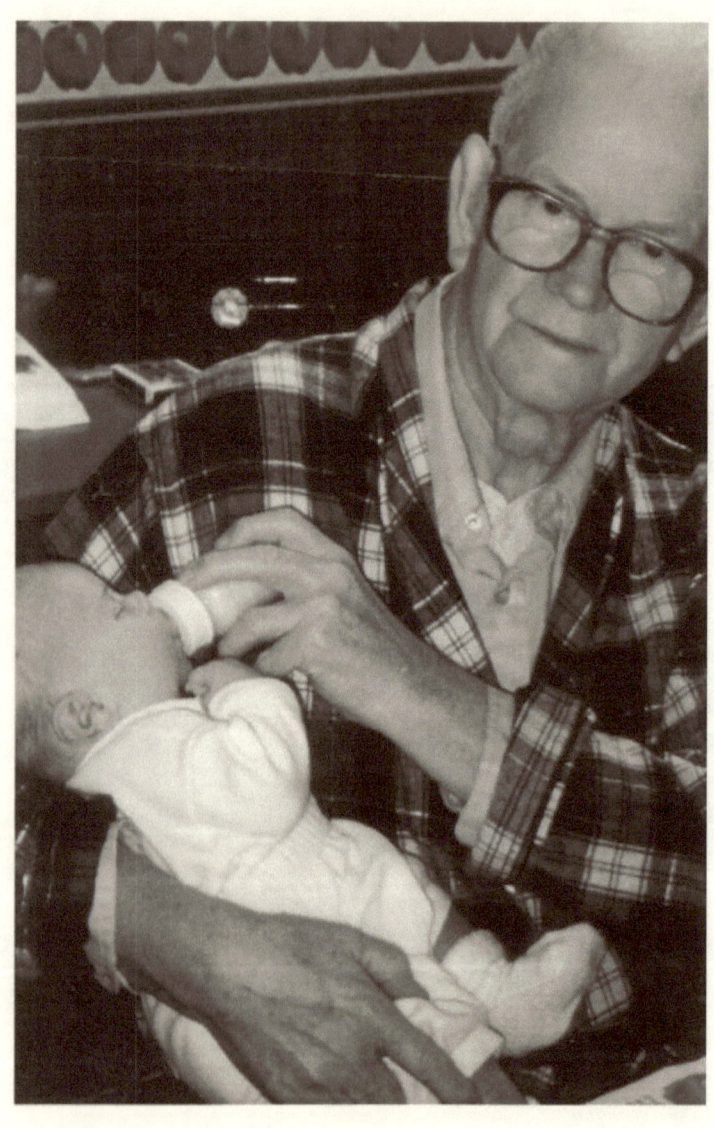

1995-Harold with great-granddaughter, Madison

Janice and Robert F. Burkhardt

New Years Eve

2015 / 2016

Jane and Harold

71st Birthday

1984

Janice 1958

3 Years Old

Orville B. Blanton

Janice's Father 1965

Born 7-18-1922 Died 6-5-1966

Mother Nellie Romeo – Blanton with Daughter Janice

1955

Nell Romeo 1940

16 Years Old

Born 2-1-1924   Died 5-27-1960

5yrs. old

Nancy Jane Milton

1955

Janice Blanton 1972

17 Years Old

Nancy Jane Milton 1968

17 Years Old

Nancy and Janice 1959

Christmas

Janice 1959

Christmas

Janice

5 Years Old

United States View Co.

Williamstown, W.V.

Milton Family

Charles, Eva, Hazel, Jewell, Myrtle, Harold and Mary

1924

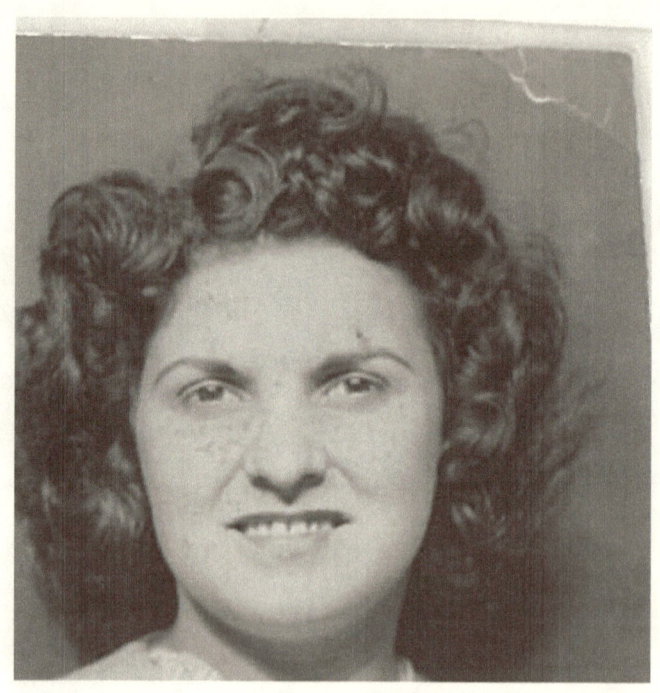

Jane Romeo 1943

Jane Romeo 1945

Jane Romeo 1937

Jane Romeo 1944

Jane Romeo 1945

Jane Romeo 1945

Jane Romeo 1945

Jane Romeo 1946

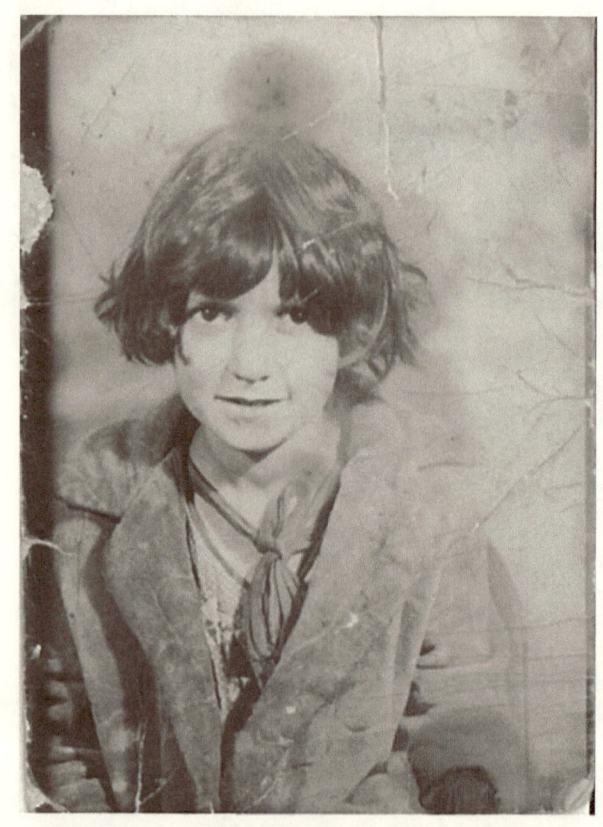

Jane Romeo 1932

Jane Romeo 1945

Nellie Agnes Romeo-Blanton

Day of Baptism

Mother Jane Romeo-Milton with Daughter, Nancy

1st Birthday

1951

Harold and Nancy 1953

Nancy and Janice 1968

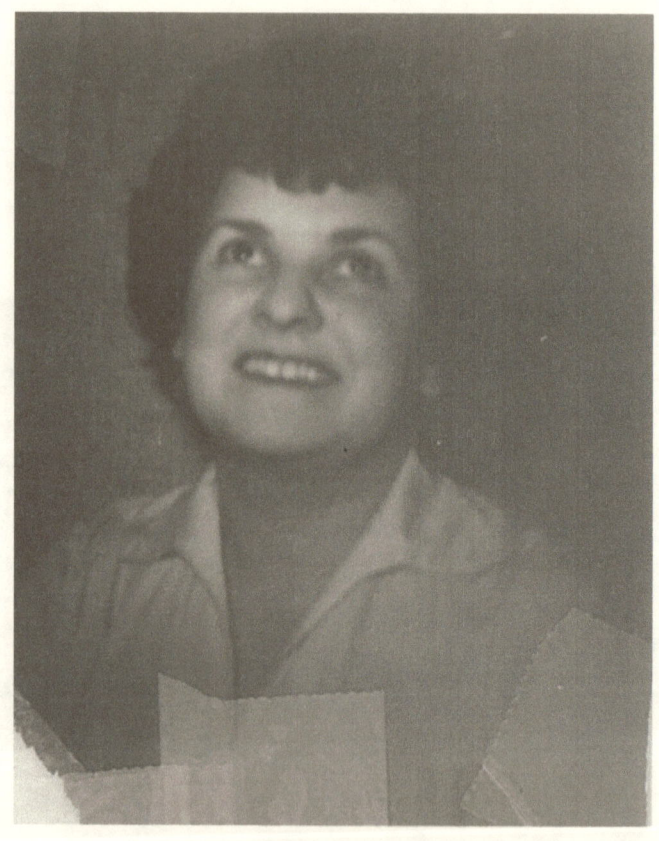

Jane Romeo 1965

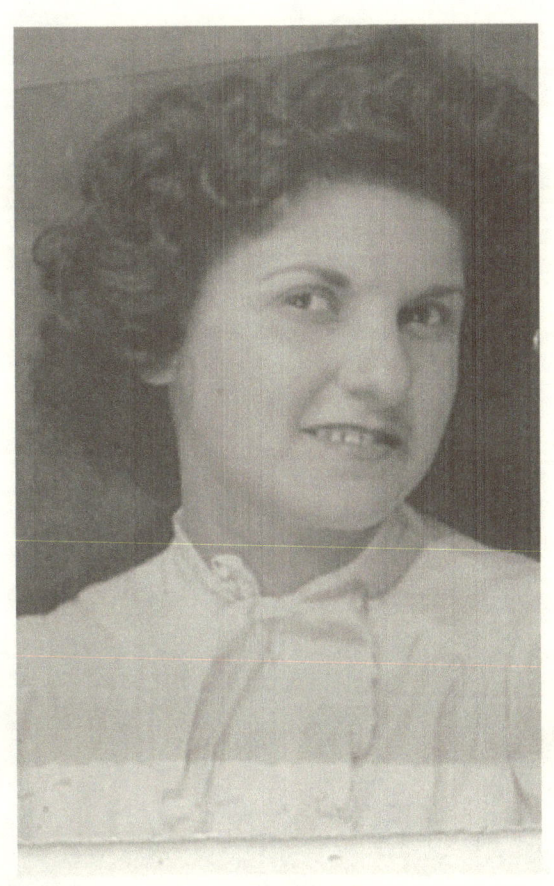

Jane Romeo 1947

Jane Romeo 1945

Jane and Harold 1951

Jane and Harold 1943

Harold 1953

Unknown, Harold, Jane, Eva, Nancy, and Unknown

1955

Nellie, Katherine, Jane, and Joe

1927

Myrtle, Mary, Charles, Eva, Unknown, and Harold

1943

Nellie Romeo

1938